# TIME IN A BOTTLE
## Women & Their Addictions

## by
# JANICE L. HALLDORSON

*AuthorHouse*™
*1663 Liberty Drive, Suite 200*
*Bloomington, IN 47403*
*www.authorhouse.com*
*Phone: 1-800-839-8640*

*© 2009 Janice L. Halldorson. All rights reserved.*

*No part of this book may be reproduced, stored in a retrieval system, or transmitted by any means without the written permission of the author.*

*First published by AuthorHouse 1/27/2009*

*ISBN: 978-1-4389-3126-5 (sc)*

*Printed in the United States of America*
*Bloomington, Indiana*

*This book is printed on acid-free paper.*

Dedicated to all the women out there still suffering alone and in silence. Know that there is hope.

# Table of Contents

CHAPTER ONE  CLAUDIA ................................... 1

CHAPTER TWO  GINA ......................................... 25

CHAPTER THREE  DIANNE .............................. 53

CHAPTER FOUR  TERRINA .............................. 79

CHAPTER FIVE  JOY .......................................... 105

CHAPTER SIX  SHILO ........................................ 129

CHAPTER SEVEN  LYLYJA ................................. 151

CHAPTER EIGHT  MIRIAM .............................. 163

CHAPTER NINE  HOLLY .................................. 181

# CHAPTER ONE
# CLAUDIA

Claudia closed the door of the apartment behind her, turned the lock, slid the chain into place and slowly got herself over to the couch where she sat down, breathing hard, without even removing the heavy wet boots and wool coat she had come in the door with. Slumped over on the edge of the couch, she put her head into her still gloved hands and starting rocking back and forth. She wanted a drink so badly she was salivating. Her mind was somehow outside of her, her body screaming demands, aching for a shot of alcohol. Her body had become accustomed to getting through the day at work without a drink; it was a controlled environment where it was easy enough to convince herself that there was no point even thinking about it, but when she got home, it was a different story. Walking through that door into the sanctity of the apartment she shared with no one, her mind went into overdrive every time.

Today was even worse than usual; she felt as though she was falling apart at the seams; the craving for a drink taking up every inch of her. Her mind was reeling; she was consumed with an overwhelming feeling of fear and contempt for everyone and everything that had ever touched her life to this point. The anti-depressant drugs she had been on for more than a decade weren't working anymore; increasing the doses had done nothing to ease the depression, and the drugs were aggravating her already damaged liver. She felt hopeless, absolutely hopeless; full of fear and anxiety; a broken spirit living in her own private hell as she rocked back and forth, head in hands, her woolen gloves soaked with tears. Claudia had stopped drinking four long years ago and here she was, on the edge of a breakdown, salivating for a drink, her mind and body going out of control.

Claudia was the oldest child in a family of six whose father abandoned them before the sixth child was born. He was a man with a gambling addiction; that's about all Claudia ever knew about him because her parents argued and fought endlessly about his gambling losses. His paycheck rarely made it past the racetrack, which caused the young family a great deal of insecurity and economic hardship, the grocery money or the rent money gambled away month after month. Every time he lost all the money betting on horses at the track he would try and sneak into the house late at night when he thought everyone would be asleep but Claudia's mother Rose would always be waiting for him and the fight would begin.

"Where's your paycheck?" she would whisper hoarsely into the darkness, trying not to wake the sleeping children.

"My paycheck is my business woman!" he would yell back at her.

By now, all the children would be startled out of their slumber with the little ones crying as Rose screamed back.

"You've been to the bloody track again haven't you! You might as well just shove that money up some horse's ass for all the good it does!" and with that she would crawl into bed with one of the kids and cry herself to sleep as her husband stormed back out into the night.

The sixth child was the last one because he disappeared one day when he went out for a pack of cigarettes and was never seen or heard from again. Life was bad enough with him but it was soon to become even worse without him. His leaving set them down a path of hardship and struggle that would impact their lives forever.

Claudia's mother Rose never re-married and carried the overwhelming burden of her large family alone. Rose suffered from undiagnosed mental illness and chronic depression, which made her an easy target for some of the sleazier characters always on the lookout for a woman to prey on. A kind word and a little attention from one of these men was a welcome respite from the grueling routine at home. Because she honestly did not know any better, she believed that these men would help her and she so desperately needed help; any kind of help. Some of them did help a bit but mostly they got what they wanted and left. Before too long, the comfort of alcohol became the best way she knew to ease her burden; make her care less; it was about the only time she ever felt anything close to good. Rose had virtually no money except what she got from the Government Relief Program and whatever these men could give her, so she did what they wanted and if they wanted her to drink; so be it. Several evenings a week, she would get herself as dolled up as she could, always wearing the same old purple dress with the same string of pink plastic pearls, a little lipstick on the cheeks and the lips, a few bobbie pins strategically placed and she was ready for action. She would leave the children home in care of the oldest child Claudia, and head out for a night at the local tavern where she would hook up with one of these men. Often, at closing time when she was sufficiently inebriated on drinks some man had paid for, she would bring him home to continue the party. They would usually bring a brown paper bag full of bottles of beer from the hotel and were so drunkenly loud that they always woke the children.

Those were the nights Claudia hated the most; sometimes she thought she would rather go to bed hungry than have to listen to some pig of a man slobbering all over her mother. Claudia always tried her best to protect the younger kids from seeing or even hearing too much. She would get up early in the morning before any of the other kids were stirring and clean up the mess from the night before; picking up bottles, emptying the overflowing ashtrays of cigarette butts, all the while trying to wake her mother out of her stupor and convince her to get the slobbering pig out of sight before all the other kids woke up. Sometimes she did and sometimes she didn't. There were times when one of these Romeos would actually stay for a few days but none were man enough to stick around long with six kids. Rose and her brood became the typical tragic family always in crisis, one disaster after another.

It didn't take more than a couple of years of life on the wild side to bring Rose to her knees. Her mental state progressed from depressions where she wouldn't get out of bed for days on end to a complete mental breakdown. She would emerge after these depressions spent in bed in a raging state of anger and begin throwing things; anything she could get her hands on without any thought of where or on whom they may land. The meager furnishings of their home became more and more battered and whoever was unlucky enough to be in the line of fire could come out with a few bruises and cuts. Claudia always hid just how incredibly scared she was from the younger ones but it was hard to hide this loud dysfunction from the neighbors and they started complaining about the kids running around with no one looking after them, getting into all kinds of trouble. Finally, someone complained to the local priest who decided to do something about it.

The priest came to visit on one of the days when Rose was incapacitated; passed out in bed with the children all over the place and out of control. The next day, the priest was back with two old nuns and they took Rose away "somewhere where they can look after her" was all they told the kids. That's all they would say; they wouldn't say where she was going or how long she would stay there or when she was coming back to be their mother again - nothing! They just stuffed her into a car and drove away leaving the two old nuns to sort out the kids and pack up their stuff.

"What's going to happen to us now?' Claudia sniffed.

"Just pack up your things and help the younger ones and hurry up about it" the old nun instructed.

The smaller children were frightened beyond reason, sobbing hysterically which appeared to really anger the two nuns. They took the two smallest children and sat them in one bedroom and closed the door while they gathered everything up. It didn't take long to round up the entire clan's bunch of tattered clothes and ratty old toys; shoving them into the two old suitcases they found under the beds. Claudia was frantic. What was happening?

"WHERE ARE WE GOING? THIS IS OUR HOME!" she shouted.

"You, young lady, had better learn to keep quiet! Back talk such as yours will not be tolerated where you are going."

"But where ARE we going?" Claudia pleaded once again.

"You are all coming with us. Your mother has been taken to a mental institution and you will probably never see her again!"

At this pronouncement, all six children began to wail and there was no stopping them. Dragging the two old suitcases, the nuns began herding the children toward the door and out into the street where there was a long black car waiting. A man in a dusty gray suit jumped out of the driver's door when he saw them approaching and opened the other three car doors while the two nuns proceeded to try and get the sobbing children into the car. The children were howling and digging their heels into the ground, flailing their arms, fighting for their very lives, but the nuns easily overpowered the children and soon had them all locked in the car, hurtling down the road toward some unknown horror.

The nuns and the driver sat in silence enduring the howls and shrieks of their small passengers as the journey continued. After what seemed like forever to the children, the car slowed to a stop in front of a huge, old gray stone building with black bars on all the windows.

"IS THIS A JAIL!!??" screamed one of the children.

"Of course not, don't be ridiculous!" snapped Sister Theresa. "It's an orphanage and it's your new home."

"BUT WE'RE NOT ORPHANS" Claudia screamed in fear and anger. "We HAVE a Mother!"

"A mother who is unfit to look after her own children! UNFIT! Do you understand what that means? We had to take you away from her because she doesn't know how to be a proper mother so now you will live here at the orphanage with all the other orphans."

The howls escalated for a few more minutes until finally, the children were starting to wear out and their loud cries turned to snuffled sobbing as they were yanked out of the car one by one and stood in stony silence staring at the place that was not a prison.

As the oldest child, Claudia had always been more or less responsible for her younger siblings and she wasn't about to hand them over now so she hung on to them as tight as she could; each one holding the hand of the next one; everyone terrified to let go. The other nun, Sister Margaret, began gesturing for them to move along; to head toward the building, but the children were frozen in panic and stood planted where they had been pulled out of the car. Sister Margaret started walking towards them and they backed up as one with her approach. The nun was not going to stand for this defiance and reached into her deep cloak pocket and pulled out a thick black leather strap and waved it in their direction.

"If you don't do what you are told, you will feel the heat of this strap, I promise you that!"

Claudia understood immediately and urged the children forward. They approached the stone steps sandwiched between the two nuns, walked up the steps and through the big doors into a dark hallway that led them eventually into an office where an even older nun sat waiting for them.

"Sit down" she ordered and they sat in the rickety, wooden chairs lined up along the wall facing the desk. "Who's the eldest here?" she asked.

Claudia stood up "It's me. I'm nine years old and the twins here are the youngest and they…."

The nun stood up. "Did I ask you who the youngest was? No I did not. Answer only the question you are asked and no more!" "I am Sister Anne and I am in charge here and you will do as I say or you will be punished. Is that understood?" No one moved a muscle. "Is that understood?" she repeated loudly.

Claudia looked down the line at the other five and jerked her head in a sign that meant do-as-I-do then looked back at the nun and nodded "Yes, we understand."

"That's yes Sister, we understand." she shouted at them.

"Yes Sister" they repeated, not quite in unison.

After all their names and birthdates had been recorded in a big green ledger book, the children were taken out of the office by either Sister Theresa or Sister Margaret one by one and shown the bunks and lockers where they were to stow their belongings. The two youngest children were put in the nursery where there were cribs and small beds with high side rails and the same dull, rough colorless blankets that were on all the beds in the orphanage. The pillows were nothing more than old pieces of blankets folded up, covered in threadbare cotton sheeting and there were no curtains on any of the high barred windows.

The children were by now in shock, and responded to the nuns' orders as if in a trance; "Stand over here, sit down, get up, put that in there, go to sleep, wake up." There was no compassion, no loving care for any of the unfortunate children who had ended up here for whatever reason. These Sisters of Mercy were not trained in childcare or nursing but were in charge nonetheless. It was ironic how unmerciful they could be; brutality and corporal punishment were the preferred methods of care. Any behavior beyond the strict guidelines of proper deportment for children resulted in beatings and punishments that no child should ever have to live through, but they did.

The children endured six long years of this loveless injustice and brutality until the authorities declared that their mother was fit to take them back into her care. Rose had been released from the mental institution almost a year before she got the children back; a period of grace in which she was to prove to the authorities that she could manage out in the world. She must have impressed them somehow, because the children were being handed back to her now. She refused to talk about where she spent those five years or what they did to her or what she had learned but the children soon found out that she had learned the art of binge drinking in the year since her release, which she had amazingly kept hidden from the authorities. Bad news for the kids but nothing could ever be as horrible as the orphanage they just left; not even a drunken mother, at least they were out of that prison.

Claudia was by now an angry fifteen year old who had hardened into a teenager who hated absolutely everyone and everything including alcohol, especially alcohol, because of what her mother's drinking had done to her and her brothers and sisters. All the children had become more troubled than ever since their time at the orphanage and there was little to rejoice at back in their mother's care. Claudia had very low tolerance for her mother's drunkenness and vowed to herself that when she grew up she would not use alcohol, not ever. This pledge of temperance lasted until her eighteenth birthday when she took her first drink of alcohol.

The vow she had sworn to never drink had somehow slipped her mind as she accepted the glass of wine from the bottle that her friends had gotten to celebrate her birthday. They didn't know about the secret temperance pledge that had conveniently slipped Claudia's mind. The wine tasted good and she liked how it made her feel all warm and tingly. After a few glasses more, life didn't seem so serious anymore; she was ten feet tall and bullet proof; a brave new woman and all the world had turned to look at her, to finally really see her as she wanted to be seen; everybody's sweetheart.

In the beginning, drinking was a welcome escape from her humdrum life; a bigger, shinier world compared to her dreary little existence. Between the ages of eighteen and twenty she embraced the socializing benefits of alcohol and drinking became something that she actually looked forward to more and more. Soon, the anticipation of getting feeling good on a few drinks turned into an intense craving and she realized something she could admit only to herself. She loved to drink. She had to drink. The more she drank the more she loved it. She loved how free she felt, how powerful and in control. And when she found Ronnie who loved to drink as much as she did, she married him.

It was a loveless match; there was nothing to bind them except the booze and that wore thin pretty fast, but they still had drunken lust in their loveless marriage and managed to produce a baby boy within the first year. The baby, of course, did not help the marriage and they spent the next twenty years trying to drink away their discontent. Drinking was about the only thing they did together; the marriage was never a happy or healthy one; Claudia felt that it was just another cross to bear. By now she had blossomed into a chronic drinker and had begun to suffer with depression even though she managed to give the appearance that her life was just fine. She felt that she was the victim in her relationship, the primary breadwinner and caregiver and the only thing she ever got back seemed to be more responsibility and bigger burdens. She knew that she did not love or respect her husband; in fact she was hard pressed to come up with anything she even liked about him. They seemed to have nothing in common except their child and the middle class lifestyle that she had worked so hard to achieve with no help from him.

It was a sorry state of existence but she had no idea how to change anything, so it stayed the same year after year. The years rolled by and nothing ever improved. If anything, Claudia and Ronnie's distaste for each other grew into hate.

By the time she was forty years old, Claudia was experiencing signs of the same mental illness and depression that her mother had, and at times, found herself unable to get out of bed for days on end. This scared her enough to seek the help of a doctor who referred her to a psychiatrist. She saw them both regularly throughout the next twelve years, all the while continuing to drink copious amounts of alcohol most days. The drinking was never brought up or questioned as a possible cause for any of her problems by either of the doctors and as the unquestioned alcohol consumption increased, so did the depression and the marriage just got worse. She was missing longer and longer stretches of time at work and, finally, in her emotional despondency, attempted suicide. She took all the anti-depressants and painkillers she could find and washed them down with a tall glass of straight vodka but somehow, it wasn't enough.

Claudia woke up in the hospital not remembering anything; couldn't even figure out where she was, until Ronnie's face came into view and it all came back to her; what she had done. He had come home from work and found her unconscious on the floor of the bathroom and called an ambulance. They rushed her to the hospital and pumped her stomach just in time, they said. It was obvious that Ronnie was more disgusted than anything and that made her wish even more that she had been able to succeed at killing herself. It wasn't enough that she was still alive, but now she had this shameful burden to bear and he wasn't making it any easier. She opened her mouth to speak but Ronnie spoke first in a loud whisper close to her face.

"Well, thanks for making such a scene! Everyone in the whole fucking neighborhood had to watch the ambulance guys haul you out of the house on a stretcher! How do you think that made me feel? Like an idiot, that's how! They're all gossiping now and I know what they're saying! They probably think I tried to kill you! Maybe you should have tried a little harder you fucking nutcase! You make me sick."

She lay there in the hospital bed wondering why she was still here. What was there to live for anyway? When they released her from the hospital the next morning, she took a taxi home to find Ronnie had cleared out. "Good riddance. Who needs the asshole" she thought to herself. For the first time in her entire life, she was alone.

The house was sold as part of the divorce settlement and they never, ever spoke another word to each other. Claudia managed to find a little apartment close enough to work that she could walk on a good day. On her own now, in the sanctity of her little apartment, her drinking escalated to even greater proportions. A mickey a day wasn't enough anymore and the half dozen shots of scotch increased to a full bottle each and every day of the week, every week. With no one to monitor how much she was drinking she could come home straight from work and drink all she wanted; no limits. On weekends she would drink from early afternoon until she passed out in the evening. She became a solitary, reclusive drinker so that as few people as possible would know about it. It was easy to avoid social events where there would be booze because she knew she might lose control; it was just easier to stay home than try and not drink around other people.

On occasion, however, she would bring her drunkenness to a public level and it was on one of these occasions that her son Ivan was prompted to intervene. Ivan and his wife had invited her to join them for dinner at a restaurant to celebrate their anniversary on a Thursday night. Claudia had actually looked forward to the outing for a change and her mood seemed to have lifted somewhat, so when she got home from work she quickly poured herself a stiff scotch and proceeded to get changed to go out. The first drink went down so smooth that she poured another as she was touching up her makeup. She finished ironing the bright blue blouse she had bought ages ago and never worn, put it on with a black skirt and actually thought she looked okay as she glanced at all the angles in the mirror. Claudia hadn't felt this good for a long time and decided to have just one more quick one while she looked through the bottom of the cluttered closet for a matching pair of black shoes.

By the time the taxi arrived, she was feeling the effects of the scotch and the taxi driver had to ask her twice for the name of the restaurant because she was slurring her words. The instant she got to the table where Ivan and his wife were sitting, they knew she was drunk. Once she had been seated, the waiter came over to take their drink orders. Ivan and his wife ordered glasses of white wine and Claudia ordered a double scotch, not catching on to the air of disapproval at the table. Happy with the anticipation of the double scotch on the way, Claudia managed a little small talk.

"So, how are you two doing? Oh, and Happy Anniversary; I didn't get you a card or anything but I'll buy you a drink."

Within minutes, the waiter appeared with their order, placed the three glasses on the table then turned to leave with a flourish. As Claudia was attempting to maneuver her hand past the water glass to reach her drink, she miscalculated and knocked the water glass over, splashing water all over the table, spilling onto Ivan's lap.

Through clenched teeth, Ivan said as sternly and quietly as he could "For God's Sake Mom, you're drunk again! I have had it with you and your drinking. Either you stop drinking or you are out of my life forever. I am sick and tired of your behavior!"

The three of them sat there in strained silence, no one moving. Claudia was the first to make a move. She was speechless as she gathered up her coat and purse and staggered out the door of the restaurant to find a taxi to take her back home again. She never should have gone, never should have left the safety of her secret little world. He knew! She didn't realize that he knew; couldn't believe that he knew. "How dare he hand me an ultimatum" she mumbled to herself as she climbed into a taxi and ordered the driver take her home. She held back the tears until she was safely behind the closed doors of her sanctuary. By the time the taxi dropped her off at home, Claudia knew in her heart that he was right, that she had to stop drinking and vowed then and there to do it. "I have to stop or I'll lose everything" she said to no one there. She couldn't lose her only son.

She sat at the kitchen table and cried till her mind began to clear and started looking through the kitchen drawers for the phone book. She found it on a chair in the corner of the kitchen, searched for the number for Alcoholics Anonymous and stared at it for a few long minutes.

When she finally managed to dial the entire number and let it ring without hanging up, someone picked up and a voice said something about Alcoholics Anonymous as she blurted out "What do I do? I have to stop drinking or my son will disown me! What do I do?"

The tears were coming again and the voice on the other end said "Would you like someone to come and talk to you? They can take you to a meeting if you like."

"Yes, yes, please tell them to come right away" she said and gave her address.

Two women arrived in less than an hour and announced that there was a meeting not far from there starting right away that they could take her to. Claudia just nodded in agreement as she put her coat back on, not saying a word. The two women talked non-stop all the way to the meeting about AA and how great it was. She just nodded back, not knowing what to say or do, feeling like a fool.

The meeting was more or less a blur of people talking but she did remember someone telling her that she should go to ninety meetings in ninety days and then she would know… know what? Whatever it was, she did go to the ninety meetings and managed to stay sober for those three months and started to feel pretty good. She felt so good that she managed to convince herself that she had done her penance and turned to her old, familiar friend, scotch whiskey once again. After all, had she not proved to herself and her son that she didn't have a problem anymore?

Claudia then proceeded to pick up where she had left off, drinking more than ever before. Over the next five years she became the woman she never wanted to be; a woman with no principles or values; chronically lying and cheating; doing whatever it took to enable her to drink as much as she needed to. She had trouble thinking clearly most of the time now because paranoia and depression had taken over. Ivan and his wife wanted nothing to do with her at all anymore, her short period of sobriety had done nothing to impress them so what was the point of not drinking. Her perverse thinking created problems with her job and she missed longer and longer stretches of work as the depression increased with the drinking. Physically, she was a mess, a very sick woman. Her blood pressure was high, her liver was enlarged, her body was bloated and puffy and her face was taking on the moon-shaped look of a chronic alcoholic. Money was always a big problem too; she was always broke, paying one credit card off with another, all the money going for booze. After that, she didn't really care.

Claudia knew from her short stint at Alcoholics Anonymous meetings that she qualified. She knew that in her heart, but her head kept denying it and she listened to her head for another five years until she got to the point where she was sick and tired of being so sick and tired. She was still seeing a psychiatrist when she finally admitted her alcoholism to both the psychiatrist and herself and understood that she could not stop drinking on her own and needed to go back to the AA meetings.

It was the spring of 1995 and it was time. She discussed the fact that she was going to stop drinking with both her family doctor and her psychiatrist who were both supportive. She knew total abstinence from alcohol was her only hope if she wanted to live, so she asked her doctor to prescribe a sedative to help her get over the first couple of weeks. Claudia was terrified of the withdrawals she could experience, deathly afraid of the possibility of delirium tremors. She planned the night she was to stop drinking and managed to find the courage to pour the remainder of a bottle of scotch down the drain of the kitchen sink. She stood over the sink with the bottle in her hand, just staring at it, afraid to open it for what might happen. What if she smelled it and couldn't control herself and took a drink? She had planned this all so well. She couldn't go back now. She held her breath as she began to unscrew the cap on the bottle and turned her face away as she poured it down the drain. When it felt empty, she turned around to replace the cap and put the bottle into the garbage can. She took one of the sedatives the doctor had given her and went to bed frightened and alone, praying to God with all her heart "Please God, help me get through this night."

The delirium tremors never came but she spent most of the nights over the next few weeks sweating and shaking. The sedatives were doing their job to some degree but she still felt extreme anxiety and on the third day of not drinking she attended an AA meeting once again. Her life was to become a routine of making it through sleepless nights to drag herself out of bed every morning to trek off to work trying to behave as if nothing was different and then attending the meetings every evening. Somehow, she managed to carry it off and before she knew it, a whole month had passed without a drink and she had progressed into a sort of sobriety once again.

This sobriety was not a healthy one however. It was strictly a physical sobriety where her body did not take in any alcohol, but emotionally, mentally and spiritually she was still a mess living in her own private hell. She was still the frightened, wounded little girl who had no faith, no coping skills and enormous anger, filled with hate and fear; unable to trust anyone, believing nothing she heard. Even though she felt contempt for absolutely everyone at the AA meetings, she kept going. The people who went to the meetings were all so sickening to her; she hated them all and she hated going to the meetings. They were always blabbing on and on about this step and that step, God this and God that. It just made her sick. Somehow though, she knew that the meetings would keep her sober so she went.

It was as though she had not given herself permission to get well. She fought and resisted anything that had to do with recovery; all suggestions were received with suspicion and denied. The hate in her heart was still growing like an insidious cancer. For a full four years she kept attending AA meetings, all the while denying herself any chance of recovery with her fearful, suspicious beliefs. Living in this constant state of fear and anxiety without her crutch was unbearable. She began to crave alcohol and constantly obsessed about drinking. Nothing much had changed for Claudia in these four years; her emotional and mental state were irrational, her physical state was terrible and her spirit still broken; living the life of a dry drunk.

So when she found herself sitting on the couch in her coat and boots with her head in her wet gloved hands, she knew she had hit her bottom even though she had not touched a drop of alcohol in four long years. At that very moment, Claudia surrendered to her alcoholism and finally admitted that she was indeed powerless over alcohol and that her life was unmanageable. Even though she had been stone cold sober for four years, she was still stumbling through her life with untreated alcoholism. All attempts to control her life were absolutely futile. She still wanted to drink more than anything else after all this time. It suddenly became clear to her that all of the doctors and their drugs could not take away her obsession to drink; could not restore her to sanity, that only a Higher Power could do that for her but only if she asked for help. It was a revelation when she finally saw it. She was not keeping herself sober. It was something much bigger than her.

All through those four years, the one persistent, nagging thought that plagued her had been to take a drink, yet she did not drink, but why? How had she resisted? She finally understood. God was doing for her what she could not do for herself and she knew it in her soul. Suddenly, she didn't feel so hopeless anymore and the tears of despair turned to tears of relief. She removed her coat and sat looking out the window feeling as though she had just woken from a deep sleep. The world didn't seem such a dark and awful place anymore. The trees were unbelievably green and the sun was shining through the branches as if it was trying to touch her. The thought came into her mind that if this Higher Power, maybe God, had actually kept her sober for these past four years, then she was prepared now to surrender her will to Him and get on with this journey of life. It must have been God who had guided her to the meetings all these years; placed her in the path of all those people and in spite of herself, she had survived. But survival wasn't enough anymore; she wanted to live and be happy for the first time in her life.

As Claudia sat there looking through the trees, she realized she needed to pray and didn't care if she felt foolish as she said out loud, "God, I am an alcoholic and I want to drink. Please help me to not take that drink. Drinking has always been the answer to my problems. I need your help God that's what I need. Please show me a miracle. Please help me" and she put her head down on the table and wept.

Something changed that day, something inside Claudia softened and she felt hope where once there had been only despair. A miracle was in fact realized that very day Claudia prayed for help. She never looked back once she understood that a power greater than herself was guiding her on the road to recovery. She went back to the AA meetings with a new attitude and found many more miracles in the fellowship. Claudia healed and grew to learn that honesty, willingness and an open mind were all she needed to succeed.

The End

# CHAPTER TWO
# GINA

A child's imagination is a powerful thing and Gina's was no exception. Summer at the cabin on the lake was always the highlight of the year and it had just become even more exciting. She had spotted a log out in the bushes behind the cabin that looked exactly like a horse. An old fallen piece of stump with gnarled branches protruding in all the right directions made it perfect for a small rider. It was hard labor for a five year old, but she managed to drag the log up to the back of the cabin where it would be ready for her whenever she wanted to ride. When she sat on it, she was transformed immediately into a princess galloping through the forest on her beautiful white horse. Lost in her make believe world she spent hours with that horse, riding it, feeding it, grooming it.

Gina played alone for the most part, watched by the birds and the squirrels. There were six older brothers who got the lion's share of attention from her mother and father so she was mostly left to her own devices. At this old cabin on the lake it was easy to have fun without anyone else. This was Gina's own personal Disneyland. She really loved spending summers at the lake where she could let her imagination run wild and just be herself, not worrying about making friends or even having friends. Life was easy there and all through the rest of her life, any time she thought of that old log horse; it would bring tears to her eyes.

Out there at the cabin was really the only place Gina ever got much of her mother's attention. Norma would take Gina out berry picking with her and the younger boys and teach them all she knew about the bugs and the trees, how to respect the weather and how to watch for storms. They would tramp through the bushes with their pails looking for wild blueberries in the summer heat, the boys complaining the whole time. Gina didn't complain; she loved doing anything with her mother and she learned to cherish nature and the outdoors from Norma's lessons. She learned about the flowers and rocks, the birds and the animals and how to watch for changes as the summer ended; how the whole forest turned bright fire red and orange in the fall. Life at the lake was so easy and uncomplicated.

But there were other kids at the lake too, of course, and as the summers went by one after the other, Gina heard them making fun of her and her family, calling them "the clan" the poor people with all the kids and no money. They laughed about the clothes they wore, especially Gina's. She was a tomboy like her mother and it never seemed to bother her to wear her brother's hand-me-down clothes. In fact, she was never comfortable in a dress or a skirt. Her mother would sew a jumper or a skirt for her and she would really try and wear it, but she felt so exposed; almost naked, and it was so uncomfortable that she would be back in the hand-me-down pants in no time.

Until she grew into a teenager it didn't matter much what she wore but as she got a little older, it started to bother her when the other kids made fun of her; the poor girl who dressed in boy's clothes. The odd time she hung around with these other kids they would always ditch her or say mean things to try and chase her away. In her mind, she felt there must be something really wrong with her for them to treat her so badly. Because of this bullying, summers at the lake became progressively more stressful, but Gina wanted so badly to be part of the group, to have friends at any cost, that no matter how mean they were, she kept coming back for more, pretending that it didn't bother her. On a good day, they would just tolerate her hanging around with them, but on a bad day they would all gang up on her and make fun of her with taunts like "Why don't you just go home tomboy. We're going for ice cream and you can't have any." Sad little Gina would shuffle off with her head hanging down, trying hard not to let the tears loose.

By the summer of her eleventh year, the bullying was out of control and Gina decided she couldn't take it anymore and made up her mind she should just die. She had heard about people dying because they took too many pills, so she waited inside the cabin pretending to read a comic book until her mother was busy doing something outside. She seized the opportunity to rummage through her mother's purse for the bottle of aspirins she knew she always kept there. There it was. She put the bottle of pills in her pants pocket and went out to the pump with an empty cup to get some water to wash them down with. Her mother was outside on the porch shelling a huge bowl of peas.

"Hi Gina, are you having a nice day?" her mother asked, glancing her way as she flipped empty pea pods into the tin pail at her feet.

"Yeah, it's okay" is what came out of Gina's mouth but inside she was screaming "Help me, please help me, everybody hates me, I just want to die!" Just as Gina took a deep breath and started to open her mouth to try and tell her mother how upset she was, one of her brothers came around the corner with a fish he had just caught.

Mom was instantly busy congratulating him on what a great fisherman he was, forgetting all about Gina. What a great feed that will be and on and on and Gina was left standing with her unspoken pain still inside. "Nobody cares about me", she thought as she fingered the bottle of aspirins in her pants pocket, "not even my own mother".

Her mother and brother walked around to the side of the cabin to clean the fish and Gina was left standing at the pump by herself. She pulled the bottle of pills out of her pocket and looked at it. It was a small bottle and not quite full but she knew her mother only ever took two at a time and pills were pills so whatever kind of pills you took, if you took more than two it should probably kill you she figured. She filled the cup with water from the pump and sat on the edge of the wooden bench nearby and put two aspirins in her mouth and quickly drank some water. They tasted horrible; really bitter, she had never had aspirins before; had never had any kind of a pill before for that matter. She put two more in her mouth and drank some more water, then looked at the bottle and decided to take two more and leave the last few in the bottle to put back in her mother's purse so no one would know how she died. She swallowed numbers five and six, scurried back into the cabin and quickly put the bottle back into the purse before her mother came inside.

There was a big flat rock on the edge of the lake where she liked to lay in the sun and watch the clouds where no one would bother her, so she decided to go there to let the aspirins do their deadly work. After about two hours of laying on the big rock in the hot sun, not even falling asleep, never mind dying, she knew it wasn't going to work. She sat up and cried, berating herself over and over again. "Loser, loser, loser, everybody hates me, I even hate me!"

Summer over, back home again, Gina felt lonelier than ever. She had no friends to talk to and just could not bring herself to talk to her mother about anything; her mother was always so dead tired; tired of raising seven kids, tired of working so hard. All of Gina's fear, anger and frustration from the bullying, the teasing and taunting started piling up inside of her, layer upon layer.

Her father Gordon was even more aloof than her mother and rarely at home. When he wasn't at work he was either golfing or curling and Mom would always excuse his absence when anyone pointed it out by saying "Your father's doing business "on the golf course" or "at the rink", whichever applied at the moment. "You know it's not all fun. It's his business, he needs to do that for work."

Gina could not understand why her Mother never seemed to get excited about going out on the odd occasions that she socialized with her husband, usually to a house party of some sort. Gina would watch her apply lipstick after she had put on the plain brown dress that she usually wore out. This was the absolute only time she ever used the lipstick. That one tube of Coral Crème lipstick must have lasted her a lifetime. At some point in the ritual, she would always mumble to herself "I'd just as soon stay home" but never once did she actually tell Gordon that she didn't want to go. It was years before Gina figured out why she never wanted to go out. Norma didn't drink; couldn't drink; half a bottle of beer and her face would light up like a red neon sign. This embarrassed her so much that she usually refused all offers of a drink or just sat there holding the same glass in her hand the entire night waiting for Gordon to get drunk enough to declare it was time to go home. He drank heavily, flirted with other women and always, always drove home. Norma would never dare suggest that he was not in a fit state to drive or she may suffer the consequences; it was better to risk crashing up the car than getting him mad at her.

Gina watched her parents carefully and felt sorry for her mother who seemed to suffer the same bullying as she did. Norma kept it all to herself though, suffering in silence, so Gina did the same. Norma's life was her family; her husband first and her children second; she was always home for them at their beck and call, cooking and cleaning but somehow, she never understood how to really communicate with any of them; especially her daughter. Gina idolized and envied her older brothers and believed everything they told her even though they grew into arrogant, womanizing men just like their father.

When one of the older brothers got married and his wife became pregnant, Gina decided to ask her new sister-in-law about babies.

"How does it get in there?" she asked, pointing to the girl's swollen belly.

The girl glanced over at Norma, grinning like she had some big secret and Norma sighed loudly, waved the girl away and took Gina by the hand. She sat Gina down in the kitchen across the table from her as she explained how a man and a woman make babies. There was a lot of pain and blood and more bleeding and then more pain as Norma described where the man puts his you-know-what and how it's a wife's duty and that was that. No mention of emotion or love or how you're going to become a woman some day or any hint of the beauty of creation. Norma had been nervously fingering a dish towel the whole time she had been administering the mother-daughter talk and the second she decided she was finished talking, she folded it lengthwise and hung it on the oven door, looked back at Gina and said "Okay?"

Gina nodded back "okay" as she pushed the chair away from the table to get up and leave the kitchen. She felt sick to her stomach and scared to death. It was horrible. A fear formed in Gina's mind that would be hard to shake.

By the time Gina was fourteen, the family had relocated to Winnipeg where Gordon had accepted a better job as an insurance adjuster. Gina had grown tall and gangly and still felt she wasn't as pretty as other girls but things got better the very first week of school. She made a friend, her first real friend. Maxine, or Max as she preferred to be called, had just moved there too so they were both new, both outsiders. Max was tough; she had a wall around her that nobody got through unless she let them in and Gina admired that about her. They became good friends in no time.

After a few weeks of checking out the kids at school, Max decided that she should have a party at her house. Her parents were rarely home and didn't really care much about what went on when they weren't there, so Max and Gina invited the coolest kids at school (the ones who drank and smoked) to the party. Most kids brought whatever they could steal from home, a few bottles of beer or part of a bottle of something or other, but Max had two full cases of beer; a whole twenty-four bottles for the party. Her parents had just had a big party the weekend before and there was lots of beer left over, so Max decided they wouldn't notice it missing. Gina had never tasted beer before but couldn't let anyone else know that, and accepted the opened bottle that Max handed her and took a sip. She liked it, and before she knew it she had polished off the bottle and was heading for another.

She had decided before the party that she was going to get drunk just to see what it was like and she succeeded. The more she drank, the better she felt; prettier, sexier and smarter but still tough enough to do whatever she wanted. It was a miracle in a bottle. She was hooked. From that party on, beer became the most important part of her social life. Nothing could be done without beer; nothing was any fun without beer. The beer drinking parties carried on right through high school and Gina was accepted as one of the crowd. Finally, what she had always wanted; she had friends.

They met in grade ten at school. Mike was painfully shy and stuttered, especially when he was nervous. He was perfect for Gina, so opposite, the good to her bad. She had been getting into a lot of trouble because of her beer drinking; she never knew when to quit and was earning a bad reputation but figured that going out with Mike would improve on that. They dated all through the rest of high school and Mike's positive influence did help Gina tame down a bit. Mike stuck by her side no matter what; even putting up with her beer drinking and right after graduating from grade twelve, they got married. She really thought she loved Mike but soon found out that nothing could compete with her love of beer.

Gina did not have a clue how to love her new husband; she had never learned to love herself so she could not possibly know how to love someone else. The low self-esteem she had suffered since childhood manifested itself now more than ever and she felt deep inside that she wasn't good enough for this man; her husband. She felt like she never measured up, and continued to drown her feelings in beer. The partying never stopped because she didn't want to stop it. She drank and carried on as if she were still single and when Mike tried to put his foot down, she would laugh in his face "You can't tell me what to do! I'll do whatever I want, it's my life!" then stay out all night just to spite him.

The death of Gina's father's two years later had a strangely profound affect on her. She slid into a depression and cried herself sick for the next six months. Even though they had never been close, the emotions she experienced after his death were just too much for her to handle. She felt so utterly out of control and began to starve herself, believing that food was the only thing in her life that she could control. The starving resulted in ulcers, which affected her drinking so she started eating again so that she could keep on drinking. When her weight ballooned from overeating, she would starve herself to feel back in control but the withdrawals from alcohol would be too much for her and she would start eating so she could drink again. It was a vicious cycle of starvation to binge drinking to overeating and back that controlled her life. She was living off the pain of not eating, the pain of overeating and the pain of alcohol abuse. The pain was all too familiar to Gina. She could not live without it anymore. It was her control, her insane sanity.

Mike hung in there for a couple more years before he left. It was too much for a regular guy to handle; there was no way to get through to Gina. He had tried everything he could think of to no avail. So here she was now all alone; embarrassed about her failed marriage;

afraid to show her face in public; feeling either too fat or too sick from drinking. Her self-esteem was at an all-time low. She knew in her heart that she did not deserve anything from anyone. She had no will to live any longer but she also knew she didn't have the guts to kill herself. When her ulcers kept her from drinking, she turned back to food again to stuff her pain and feelings deep down where she could never feel them again. The loneliness, the hurt, the shame; push them all down with doughnuts and pastries, pizza after pizza, anything would do, until she would be in a kind of a stupor and fall asleep; never satisfied or satiated but numb, so she kept stuffing. She had moved back in to her mother's house and it was easy to hide there; no one bothered her, least of all her mother. In less than four months she had gained almost eighty pounds. She wanted to die, to eat herself to death. She had always had a poor body image of herself, but now she really hated herself and refused to allow anyone to see her.

She ordered food from the restaurants that would deliver and her mother shopped almost every day from the list Gina would leave on the kitchen counter at night. Her mother never questioned the list; never complained about the money she was spending; hauling in the bags of frozen cakes and pies, the bags and bags of potato chips and dips, the cheesecakes from the bakery, the boxes of cheap chocolates. Whatever was on the list, Norma bought and never said a word. She knew Gina was hurting and she did not know what to do about it except to let her be and get her what she wanted.

She thought she was helping.

They didn't talk about anything; neither of them knew what to say to the other. Gina was intent on eating herself to death and Norma was, in her mind, doing all she could to help her daughter feel better. Norma had no idea that she was enabling Gina's food addiction. Gina had no friends left; Maxine had moved to the west coast a couple of years before and since then, Gina had alienated pretty well everyone she knew. If anyone did phone, she wouldn't talk to them anyway.

Max hadn't been back to Winnipeg for two years so when she came back to visit her parents she decided to look up a few old friends and called Norma's place trying to locate Gina. When Norma heard Max's cheerful voice, she decided to tell her the truth about Gina instead of the usual response of "Sorry, she's not here right now, can I take a message?" even though she was always there. She knew she couldn't lie about this any longer.

"Oh, Maxine, Gina is in a terrible state" she said as her voice started quivering. "She has been hiding out here ever since Mike left her. She won't talk to anybody; she doesn't even leave the house. I think she's trying to eat herself to death!" As she said the words out loud she realized for the first time how very worried she actually was. She had just been going through the motions not knowing what to do but now that she had said it, she seemed to gain some strength. "Maxine, can you help her please? She needs a friend right now."

Maxine hadn't spoken a word on the other end of the phone. She was stunned. She had never thought of Gina as someone who would fall apart like this. She had always seemed so tough and in control when they used to party together in high school.

"Yeah sure, of course I'll help. I'll be there just as soon as I can."

"Oh, thank you Maxine, come quickly please."

Norma looked around nervously as she hung up the phone. She had been speaking as quietly as she could so that Gina would not hear her doing the unthinkable, inviting someone over to see her. Norma looked around the corner, down the hallway. Good, Gina was in her room with the door closed and the television turned on so loud that she couldn't have heard her talking to Max on the phone. She knew how mad Gina would be if she knew that she had invited one of her friends over to see her. Nobody was supposed to see her, ever! Not for any reason. That was the order she had given Norma.

The doorbell rang about an hour later and Gina jumped; "I didn't order anything, who could that be?" She got off her bed, turned down the volume on the TV and stood by her closed door listening. She heard her mother opening the front door and then closing it again. "Probably some kid selling magazines or something" she thought to herself as she turned the TV volume back up.

When she heard her bedroom door open, she turned around to see what her mother wanted but it wasn't her mother, it was Max! Gina's first response was anger. No one was supposed to see her like this.

She looked Maxine in the eye and asked her "What are you doing here? I thought you moved to the coast?"

"Good to see you too Gina!" Maxine replied. I came to visit my folks for a few days and wanted to catch up with you."

"Yeah, well there's nothing to catch up on here so if you don't mind, I don't really want any company" Gina said to the television.

"Well, yeah I do mind Gina. That's no way to treat an old friend. It looks like you're going through a rough time and maybe I can help."

"You can help me by leaving me alone." Gina said as she turned to face Maxine.

"I don't think I can do that Gina. Let me help you. Talk to me. Tell me what's going on."

Norma backed out of the room and shut the door quietly behind her, silently thanking God for sending Maxine.

"I heard about how you and Mike split up; I'm really sorry that it didn't work out for you guys Gina, but look, it's not the end of the world okay?"

Gina had turned her back on Maxine and was staring at the television screen. She couldn't decide how she felt. One part of her was screaming "Get her out of here now! No one can see me like this!" and the other part was hoping that she wold stay and talk to her because she was so very lonely, but she hadn't associated with anyone for so long she didn't know how to start. She was so self-conscious of how she looked. None of her clothes fit her anymore. All she could fit into were the oversized t-shirts that she used to wear as night shirts with a pair of baggie, grey sweats that her mother had brought home for her one day from who knows where. Suddenly she was conscious of the old, faded T-shirt with the big cartoon puppy on the front. The seam down the right side had come undone a few inches from the bottom, but up until this moment, she hadn't even noticed the hole that now she couldn't keep her finger out of.

She felt so uncomfortable, running her hand through her hair, wondering how she must look to Maxine standing there looking so together in her nice jeans and suede jacket. Maxine sensed her discomfort and walked up behind her and put her hand on Gina's shoulder.

"It's going to be okay you know. It really is. I'll do whatever I can to help you get through this."

Gina's head dropped to her chest and the tears started falling to the floor. She sobbed silently like that for a moment then turned her body around to face Maxine without lifting her face up and Maxine held on to her till she finished crying. Finally, she raised her head.

"Oh Max, I am so afraid and lost, I just don't know what to do."

"You have to start living again Gina. There's a whole world out there and I'm here for you, so let's have some coffee and talk about it."

After Gina washed her face and found a more presentable T-shirt to put on, she came out to the kitchen where Max was sitting with the coffee Norma had made for them. Gina told Max all about the problems with her marriage to Mike and how she had started going out and partying because she couldn't deal with Mike's constant bitching about her drinking. She just needed to get away and be herself; how it was partly his fault that she had been partying and how it was all his fault that he just couldn't handle it and how drinking wasn't even the problem anyway. She hadn't touched a drink for months now, so how could that possibly be a problem by any stretch of the imagination? Wasn't it all so ridiculous and unfair to her?

But yes, she had to admit that food had become her biggest problem since she had holed up at her mother's house and shut herself off from the rest of the world. She couldn't stop eating; it was all she could think about every waking minute. Food had become a complete obsession. She was ashamed of her behaviour and embarrassed by her appearance. At first she had lied to her mother about how much she was eating but soon got over that and didn't care anymore because she needed her mother to keep her supplies stocked.

Max decided this was something they could work on. An exercise program and a diet, that's all she needed. Gina was immensely relieved that Max thought there was hope for her. With Max's help and encouraging phone calls over the next six months, she lost most of the weight she had gained and got a job working in a warehouse where she could keep in shape. She filed for a divorce from Mike and moved out of her mother's house into her own place. Everything seemed okay on the outside but on the inside, things were still a mess. She thought she had the food under control by keeping herself on a strict diet but her emotions were still all over the place. Physically, she felt better than she had in a long time. Her ulcers weren't bothering her now so she decided it was safe to have a couple of beer to calm herself down. After all, she was eating properly so what could it hurt?

Maxine had kept in touch when she went back to the coast but it still wasn't the same as having someone around to talk to so she started hanging around the bars again. It felt so good to be back in the bar world again; the familiarity of it all; the smell, the dimness, the music and the men who paid attention to her. She soon found herself at the bar every night and met Vince who was there every night as well. The beer went down real easy with a drinking companion like Vince.

Vince liked his beer as much, if not more, than Gina and they soon became an item. In no time at all, Vince had moved right in to Gina's place, which was just fine with her. This was the cure for loneliness. The next few years flew by as they drank, fought and made up a thousand times over. Finally, Gina decided she needed to get married and be responsible so she could have babies. She offered Vince an ultimatum and in a drunken stupor, he agreed. Gina had herself husband number two. She really, really thought that getting married and pregnant would solve everything. She got pregnant with no problem and did the right thing; she quit drinking so that no harm would come to the unborn child. Pregnancy was enough motivation to keep her sober throughout the entire nine months and then into nursing the baby once it was born, keeping her weight under control with her strict diet. Before she had weaned the baby, she found herself pregnant again, so she stayed sober for three busy years. Her fluctuating weight over the three years drove her crazy though, and forced her to alternate her strict diet with bingeing and purging in between the pregnancies to try and keep the weight down. She was terrified to gain back the weight she had lost and obsessed about it constantly.

Once the second baby had been weaned, she knew what came next. She could drink again and release herself from the lonely life of a sober wife married to an alcoholic. She picked up right where she had left off, expecting to cure the loneliness and pain that she had endured for the sake of her babies.

Most of the time she felt as though she was torn right down the middle; love him, hate him, eat, starve, drink, don't drink; each day more insane than the last. She tried hard to live a normal life being a good mother and a good housekeeper. In fact, her housekeeping was over the top. She thought if she kept the house clinically clean, that would make her life good and orderly. She went through the motions every day with the same exact routine and once supper was all ready on the stove, would stand at the front door and wait for Vince to arrive home from work. When he would pull into the driveway in his truck and come up the sidewalk with that familiar case of beer in his hand, her heart would sink; tonight would be like every other night. Weeknights were always the same, case of beer and television. They would drink and fight. Weekends they would go out to the bar or a house party and get drunker still. The more Gina drank, the sicker she felt, the angrier she got and the more they fought.

Gina still went out on her own once in a while and one night decided to find a man to console herself with. She had needs, she reasoned, which were not being met, and here was a guy who was more than willing to help her out so she started what was to become an affair with this man. Years later, she decided the affair was one of the biggest mistakes she had ever made. When she would come home from being with that man, she could hardly even hug her kids; these perfect little innocent children who did not deserve this dirty person as a mother. The affair ended, but the self-loathing and guilt that it caused lasted for the next fifteen years. When the affair ended, Gina and Vince went for counseling but nothing changed and she ended up leaving with the two kids and filing for a divorce.

Gina and the kids were on their own for about six months when she bottomed out. She had been drinking heavily and couldn't even go to the grocery store without having a drink first. Her old ways were reappearing just like they were never gone. On weekends, she would get a babysitter and hang out at the sleaziest bar she could find just so she could feel better about herself when she looked around, thinking that she wasn't that bad, but in reality, she was really no different than the rest of them.

One Sunday morning she found herself naked in the bed of a house she had never seen before. It was a run down dump of a place; nothing was familiar and she couldn't remember anything about how she had gotten there or who she had been with, but she knew that she had been violated. She was devastated. "Oh my God, what have I done?" she whispered to herself. Thoughts were racing through her muddled brain. "What did I do?" She couldn't even bear thinking about it she was so disgusted with herself. She was feeling sicker by the minute trying to sort it all out. She gathered her clothes up off the floor on the other side of the room, quickly pulled on her jeans and shirt without taking the time to find her underwear, went through the next room and out the front door hoping no one saw her. There didn't seem to be any life in the house, which was a relief. She got outside and started walking as fast as she could; it didn't matter where; just away from here. Her purse had no money in it which was nothing unusual after a night at the bar but it meant that she had to walk all the way home which seemed to take forever. She had never felt so low in her life and all she could think about now was getting home and out of sight.

When she finally made it to her front door, she could hardly breathe; the fear had such a hold on her. She was so angry with herself for having let this happen. She wrote a check for the babysitter because she had no cash and the babysitter smiled and said thanks; she didn't usually make that much for a night's babysitting. Gina got the kids and sat them in front of the TV with bowls of cereal and ran into the bathroom. She didn't want the kids to know that she was upset so she stood behind the bathroom door and stuffed the towel hanging there in her mouth to muffle her agony. Inside she was screaming but it was more like a moan coming out of her throat into the towel.

Suddenly, she fell to her knees and from the very depths of her soul silently cried "Help me God! Please help me!" She kept repeating her short prayer as thoughts of suicide went racing through her mind. Just then, the phone rang. "Okay, get yourself together, answer the phone" she said out loud. She wiped her face hard with a dry towel and ran through the living room to get the phone in the hallway. The kids hadn't noticed anything; they were still glued to the cartoons on TV, slowly eating their bowls of cereal.

"Hello" came out all wobbly into the phone.

"Gina, you sound funny, what's wrong?"

It was her mother. Gina couldn't talk; couldn't get the words out; she was trying but it was more like gasping and her mother instinctively knew she needed help.

"I'll be right there. Don't do anything. Just go sit in the kitchen. I'll be right over."

And she was. She must have been speeding all the way because she was there in record time and Gina was waiting just as she had ordered, sitting in the kitchen. Her mother got her calmed down to where she could speak coherently and the whole story came flooding out. How she had been drinking at this bar and couldn't remember anything and woke up in some ramshackle old house with no clothes on and how she had walked home this morning and how all she wanted to do was die, just die. She couldn't stand it anymore; she hated herself so much; everyone must hate her even more!

Her mother reassured her that she loved her and suggested calling her family doctor so she did. She told him that it was urgent she see him right away and he made room for her on his schedule. Her mother stayed with the kids while she went to the doctor. The doctor quickly decided that he was not the one to help her; she needed to see a psychiatrist. The appointment was made for the next afternoon. Gina sent her mother home reassuring her that she would be okay. Actually, she needed a drink and knew she couldn't possibly drink with her mother there after what she had just told her, so she waited till the kids were asleep and polished off a six pack of beer before she passed out on the couch.

The next morning she dropped the kids off at school with lunches so they wouldn't have to come home. She then went home and back to bed, feeling utterly exhausted and knowing that she could not show up at this appointment with booze on her breath. She set the alarm for 1:00 p.m. so she could make the 2:00 p.m. appointment. Sleep came mercifully and she woke with a start as the alarm went off. She took a long shower, wanting to smell clean and dressed as seriously as she could; black pants and a grey shirt; no color; normal, normal, nothing to give her away. This was not a crazy woman here.

After about thirty minutes of questions during which the shrink had been taking copious notes, he announced that it was obvious to him that first of all, she was an alcoholic and secondly, she was suffering from bipolar manic depression. She would need treatment for the alcohol addiction and a prescription to deal with the depression in the meantime.

After he finished speaking, she looked him straight in the eye and said "No, I'm not, I am not an alcoholic! I can quit anytime I want to. I've quit lots of times before."

As the words hit the airwaves and circulated back to her brain, she realized what she had just said. The thought came into her mind what she had heard somewhere long ago that the definition of insanity is doing the same thing over and over and expecting a different result. Yes, that was what she had been doing and here she was sitting in a psychiatrist's office defending her insanity.

Before the shrink had a chance to say another word, she said quietly "Okay, I'll try it, maybe I am an alcoholic, but I don't want the drugs. I just want to be normal. No drugs." The doctor was hesitant that she not take the drugs but seeing how determined she was, agreed that AA meetings would be a place to start.

"Let's just see how it goes" he offered.

She left the doctor's office without the prescription and very little optimism. Just as she had promised the shrink, she called an old friend who she knew had been in AA to see if he could take her to a meeting. The so-called friend was more than happy to take Gina to the meeting but had more than meetings on his agenda and she had to disassociate herself from him quickly. This was a life and death situation for Gina. If she didn't sober up and be a proper mother to her kids, who was going to look after them? Their father was useless, they couldn't depend on him for anything, so that left her and she was on the fast track to becoming useless as a parent herself.

Gina was astounded at what she found when she walked into the AA meeting. Here were all kinds of people, normal looking people, smiling and welcoming her with a handshake or a hug. She sat down with the rest of them and by the time the hour was up, knew hope for the first time in her life even though she didn't know a soul. It was okay now, she belonged here; she really did fit in, and she grabbed onto the recovery program like it was her last chance at life. Her commitment paid off in miracles. These were the kind of miracles that didn't come out of a bottle. For the first time in her life she did everything she was told to.

It took a good five years to lift the fog that she had been in and another five years before she began to see who she really was. All her life she had been doing what she thought she needed to do but never really knew why. She learned that her emotional growth had stalled when her addictions began, so she actually had an emotional age of fourteen. The twenty years that had passed since then were void of normal emotional growth. With a lot of hard work, tears and heartache, Gina grew into a respectable adult and a responsible mother. Once her sobriety was secure, she began attending workshops on self-love and acceptance and sought counseling to dig through all the issues. It quickly became clear that she had to deal with her food addiction as well as the alcohol addiction, and she was able to do so in the same healthy way using the Overeaters Anonymous program to achieve the healthy mind and body that she has today.

As Gina matured and grew in recovery, her self-esteem grew with her. She went back to school to enable her to get a better job and eventually bought a house of her own. She earned back her self-respect and peeled off the guilt and shame she had carried around for a lifetime. Today, her friends are the people she has met through the recovery programs. These have been the best years of her life and have given her the gift of contentment.

The End

# CHAPTER THREE
# DIANNE

Dianne woke up coughing and choking in a room filled with smoke. She looked around, saw the familiar pots and pans hanging from the racks above her and realized she was still at work in the kitchen of the restaurant. The smoke alarm was blaring and there was a fire fighter looking directly into her eyes.

"Can you hear me?" he asked. Dianne nodded in the affirmative.

"I'm going to help you get out of here so just lean on me now" he said as he gently lifted her arm to rest on his shoulder, pulled her up and half carried her out of the smoldering kitchen.

The fire fighters determined that there wasn't actually any fire; just a lot of smoke coming from the grill which had been left on after the restaurant closed hours before. But if the smoke alarm hadn't gone off, it could have been much worse. The firemen insisted on sending Dianne to the hospital in an ambulance to make sure she was all right. She had, after all, inhaled a lot of smoke. She felt dazed and confused on the way to the hospital; her husband Michael had arrived just after the fire fighters but he wasn't with her in the ambulance.

Michael got to the hospital some time later and when the doctors assured him that Dianne was going to be fine and that she could go home, he brought the car around to pick her up.

He was angry. "What are you trying to do? Burn the whole restaurant down?" he shouted at her. "This is going to cost me a lot of money! Do you know how much it is going to cost to fix the kitchen? And our insurance will go up! This is a disaster. Oh my God, the bad publicity we'll get!"

Dianne stared out the car window, not saying a word. There were no words to defend herself with; she couldn't actually remember exactly what had happened yet. The tirade went on as Michael continued berating her all the way home. When the car finally pulled into the garage at their home, she got out and walked silently into the house straight to the bathroom where she locked the door behind her and sat down on the edge of the tub and cried. She was used to him treating her badly so that wasn't what brought on the tears. She was crying because she felt so lost and alone. Her husband had shown no concern for her; only for his beloved restaurant and that hurt. After a few minutes of sitting there on the cold enamel edge of the tub, she stood up unsteadily and slowly removed her clothes, turned on the shower to hot and stepped in, closing the glass doors behind her, hoping to wash away the stench of the fire she had somehow caused.

As the water pelted down the back of her neck, it all started coming back to her. She remembered staying at the restaurant after everyone had left for the night to work on a menu for a wedding party coming up the next month. She was tired, but she liked being there alone sometimes and it was an excuse to not go home. She must have taken too many pills. Sometimes she miscalculated and took too many antidepressants and lately she had been taking a lot of painkillers. She remembered feeling a little shaky, kind of woozy as she lit a cigarette, but she hadn't eaten all day except for a diet shake and shrugged it off as hunger. The exhaustion she felt was overwhelming; she hadn't been sleeping well for weeks; it seemed there weren't enough sleeping pills to make her fall asleep anymore. She tried to visualize what happened next, but it was just a blur. The fire department concluded the cause of the alarm was carelessness resulting in smoke damage and that she was a very lucky woman. What did they know?

Dianne was the oldest of three children born into a very traditional Greek family. Her parents Nico and Anastasia had come to Montreal right after they had been married in Greece. They came to work in a restaurant that Nico's family had already established until they could afford to start their own business. They worked hard and built up the business quickly, becoming successful restaurateurs in their own right. As soon as Anastasia started having babies, her mother came from Greece to live with them and look after the children while Anastasia and Nico worked at the restaurant. Grandmother became the main caregiver; the children hardly ever saw their parents. Nico was a binge drinker and compulsive gambler who showed up at home only to change his clothes and maybe sleep a little, whereas Anastasia never drank but relied on prescription drugs to get her through the busy days and the never-ending nights. Nico's gambling at the casinos was legendary; he was a four-star regular and they fought about money a lot; especially the fact that Nico sent money home to his family in Greece, which drove Anastasia crazy. Anastasia was paid for her work at the restaurant, but it was never nearly enough to pay for the expensive lifestyle she had developed. She was always short of money; her paycheck was always too small and she was constantly asking her father for money, which made Nico furious.

When the children were old enough to be on their own, their Grandmother moved to a house down the street, having had enough of the fighting, so the children ended up at Grandmother's house all the time because there was no one at home when they needed them. Dianne never felt that she really had a home; it was always back and forth, back and forth, sleeping here one night, there the next; always looking for books and clothes that ended up being at the "other" house. It was only when they were old enough to help out at the restaurant that they really began to know their parents.

Nico was a typical Greek father, strict but not mean or physically abusive. Anastasia, however, was not so typical; she did not seem to have any maternal instinct and would have been fine with not having any children; she had never really wanted them, truth be told. Anastasia was a social butterfly; dressed to the nines in the most beautiful, expensive clothes, makeup and jewelry, concerned far more with her appearance than with her own children.

Dianne was her father's favorite and she knew it from a very young age. To please him, she tried her best to be the perfect child in any way she could. She was twelve years old when she started to help out at the restaurant. It was her only social life; she had no friends to speak of and didn't participate in any extracurricular activities at school. Even into her teens, she kept to herself, didn't date or go to dances or do any of the other things teenage kids usually do. She was content to do whatever it was that her father wanted her to do; her life's purpose was to please him. She excelled in school because that made him happy. When her parents went to Las Vegas to gamble as they often did, Dianne looked after her younger siblings and worked at the restaurant without complaint. She did nothing to disappoint her beloved father and she could do no wrong in his eyes. They went as a family to weddings and parties and the children were treated for the most part as adults at any social functions once they were teenagers.

Dianne never felt attractive like her mother. Anastasia was tall, slim and beautiful. Dianne felt homely and fat and it didn't help when her father would point out that his little princess was getting fatter all the time. That really hurt, not pleasing him, but she still preferred her father over her mother, even when she caught him cheating with the nineteen year old housekeeper they had brought over from Greece to work in their home.

Dianne came home early from school one day when both her parents should have been at the restaurant and heard muffled voices coming from the master bedroom which her parents shared. Something was not right. She crept up to the door and listened with one ear as close as she dared. She couldn't make out the words and the curiosity was killing her, so she took a chance and crouched down on her hands and knees and peered under the bottom of the door where there was a slit of space she could just barely see through. Without making a sound, she peered into the crack, into the darkness. After a few seconds her eyes adjusted to the dimness of the room and she could make out the shapes of two people in the room; two bodies on the bed. She knew her father immediately, after all, she had expected to see him in there, but the other shape shocked her so much she stopped breathing. It was Helena, the housekeeper, naked on her mother's bed! She pressed a hand over her mouth fearing that a scream would come out and backed up as fast as she could still on her hands and knees down the hallway to her own room. She got to her room and stood up, head reeling from the shock of what she had just seen. There was no way she could stay there knowing what was going on down the hallway, so she ran out of the house and kept running till she couldn't run anymore. When she caught her breath, she decided she had to talk to someone but who? Aunt Nina. She knew she had to tell someone before she exploded. Aunt Nina would know what to do. Well, Aunt Nina told her to let God sort it out; that she should leave it alone and just forget about it but she could not.

It was all she could think about; the image of her father and Helena on her mother's bed; she obsessed about it all through the night. The next day was a Friday and she knew her father always gambled at the casino on Friday afternoons, so she went there to confront him. He was more than a little surprised to see Dianne at the casino but did not question her when she asked him to step outside for a minute with her.

He looked quizzically at her as she said "I know what you are doing with that girl Helena!"

"What I do is none of your business" he said very calmly as a flush crept up his neck to his face. He seemed more embarrassed than angry and dismissed Dianne abruptly, telling her to go home and forget about such nonsense as he turned and walked back into the casino.

Meanwhile, Aunt Nina had clued Anastasia in to her husband's deceit and she was dealing with it in her own way. Anastasia had taken the news without emotion; had simply walked up to Helena, slapped her hard across the face and told her to get out of her house. Helena never came back to the house but Nico gave her a job at the restaurant and no one said a word, no one.

After that incident, Anastasia never trusted Nico again for a minute. She was always sending Dianne or one of the other kids to check on him, spy on him, check the mileage on his car, follow him, listen in on his phone calls, having someone reporting his whereabouts at all times. Nico and Anastasia moved into separate bedrooms and never slept together again even though they kept up the public appearance of a married couple. They still socialized as a couple, but always with Dianne or one of the other kids, never just the two of them. Consequently, Dianne spent a lot of her teenage years in nightclubs with her parents; Anastasia never wanted to be caught alone with her husband again.

When Dianne turned twenty-one, her parents decided to send her to Greece for a holiday as a graduation gift. She had worked hard and graduated with a degree in psychology. In preparation for the holiday, she starved herself to lose thirty pounds and felt pretty good about how she looked for a change. The family in Athens threw her a big party when she arrived and she met Tomas. Tomas' mother was a servant to Dianne's family in Athens. He seemed like a really nice guy and for the first time ever, she thought she actually had feelings for a man. They became friends despite the language barrier; he did not speak a word of English and she did not speak Greek. Dianne was absolutely terrified of sex so the relationship never got intimate and all too soon the holiday was over and she was on her way back to Montreal.

Tomas kept in touch with lovely letters all written in Greek which she had to have her mother or Aunt Nina translate for her and which she replied to every time. But the problem was that they all disapproved of Tomas; the whole family was against him. He wasn't good enough for them; they were better than everyone else, especially according to her grandmother who would just make a "psssssh" sound whenever Dianne would mention his name. The letter writing went on back and forth for over a year until Dianne returned to Greece with her grandmother. She was absolutely forbidden to see Tomas again but could not help herself. She snuck away from her grandmother and spent two nights with Tomas; two innocent nights where nothing sexual happened between them at all.

Grandmother found out about their tryst and declared "If you do not phone him and say goodbye forever I am not coming back to Canada with you. He is a lowly laborer and you are educated and above his place. I forbid!"

Dianne knew she could not be held responsible for her grandmother's not returning to Canada, so dutifully obeyed the command and did not answer Tomas' calls for the rest of the time they were in Athens. Meanwhile, she consoled herself by going out with her cousins to the nightclubs and met Michael.

Dianne had been back in Montreal for about a month when one of her aunts in Athens telephoned to say that Michael wanted to come to Canada to marry her. Everyone agreed that Michael was a much better match than Tomas and encouraged Dianne to pursue this proposal.

"Well, good, somebody wants me; that is kind of nice, and at least I can understand him, he does speak English" she thought to herself as she packed her bags for Greece once again. Back in Athens, they spent two weeks meeting every day; very proper, always with a chaperone in tow and got engaged without ever actually getting to know each other. Dianne's parents sponsored Michael's entry into Canada and put him to work in their restaurant immediately upon his arrival.

Three days before the wedding, Dianne decided it was all a big mistake, she didn't want to marry Michael. She told her grandmother first and then told Michael. He took it hard. He got drunk and took a gun out into a field threatening to kill himself, but he didn't. Grandmother talked him out of it by promising him that Dianne would indeed, marry him, that she was just nervous, not to worry, she would take care of it and she did.

They went through with the wedding ceremony; Dianne sulked and Michael got drunk. The marriage was a lousy one; their sex life was almost non-existent and he started cheating on her before long. They lived in a small apartment building on a hill overlooking the river and at least once a week, every single week, Dianne would walk across the bridge over the river to her lawyer's office to ask for a divorce. Michael would follow behind her all the way there and the lawyer would tell her the same thing every week.

"You don't have grounds for a divorce. Being unhappy is not grounds for a divorce".

Michael always vehemently denied any accusations that he was committing adultery, case closed, and they would walk single file back across the bridge again, still married.

At the end of the first year of the troubled marriage, Dianne had a complete nervous breakdown and ended up in the hospital where she was shocked to find out she was pregnant. Her mind had been set on going back to Greece to find Tomas but that was impossible now. While she was pregnant, Dianne discovered that Michael had been having an affair with a married woman who had been a friend of theirs, so as soon as the baby Alexander was born, Dianne secured a prescription for anti-depressants, took the new baby and moved in with her grandmother. This seemed to twig something in Michael and he came begging for a second chance. Dianne agreed to try and make it work as a family. They bought a new house and attempted to make it a home if for no other reason than for the child.

Michael had done well in the restaurant business and was already partnering up with the family in three other restaurants now. Dianne was soon back working at the restaurant during the day leaving their baby boy at home with a nanny. Even though it was a huge part of her life, the restaurant never really felt like "hers" or even partly "hers" because she was never included in any decision making; never knew what was going on financially or any other way for that matter. She was treated more like an employee than an owner. They had a beautiful home where she cooked and cleaned and polished the shoes and laid out the clothes; played the role of a good wife but felt no ownership. Michael and Dianne did not know how to communicate with each other and as their son grew, Dianne found out that she didn't know how to communicate with him either.

She took out a lot of anger and frustration on their only child, pushing him to excel in school when he got older; always telling him "God is going to punish you" when he disappointed her, constantly threatening to send him to a juvenile detention home if he didn't do better. She hated her life more and more every day and she would pray to God and ask "Why am I being punished so?" In desperation to feel better, she started seeing a psychiatrist who put her on more anti-depressants but she was still unhappy and frustrated and tried to ease her pain with food; eating to cheer herself up until she was sick. She never drank at home so food was her main solace when the pills just didn't do it. She started double and triple doctoring; getting prescriptions for painkillers for back pain from several doctors because one would never give her enough. By now, it would take at least seven or eight pills at a time to get the relief she needed.

Dianne's name was on their joint checking account for the purpose of running the household but she wrote lots and lots of checks for whatever she wanted. Michael would threaten to take her name off the account but she knew that her father would kill him if he cut her money off so she wasn't the least bit worried. She made out a lot of checks to Cash so she could play bingo, which could get expensive. By now, she was totally and completely dependent on prescription drugs and seriously addicted to gambling in the form of bingo. Michael couldn't take it anymore and confronted her one night as she was coming in from a late night of bingo.

"Dianne, we need to talk. Look, it's pretty obvious we don't love each other anymore or if we ever did, so why not just live separately?"

Just as she was about to open her mouth to protest that she was not leaving her home he interrupted with "Just wait, we can still both live here, just not together in the same room. Maybe it will help. What do you think?"

She was tired, "Sure, why not."

That night, he moved all his things into the spare bedroom. They were still living together and working together and it seemed to be tolerable until Dianne found out that he was sleeping with Rhonda, one of the new waitresses at the restaurant. This was not supposed to happen anymore; it was such a slap in the face. No wonder he wanted separate bedrooms. She confronted him, but of course he denied it all. She started following him around, leaving the house in the middle of the night; leaving Alexander alone in the house; out in the night air walking the streets in her housecoat three blocks over to see if his car was parked at her house. Rhonda the whore, Rhonda the bitch. She was consumed with rage and didn't know what to do about it. She would scream obscenities at Michael in frustration and poor little Alexander heard it all. The worst of it was that she had to work with Rhonda at the restaurant day in and day out seeing that smiling, smirking face. Dianne hated Rhonda so much it almost killed her and she lived with this hatred every minute of every day. Her life had become an unbelievable replica of her parents' life.

Three years later, still on the anti-depressants and painkillers and fifty pounds overweight, she went to see yet another doctor who gave her a prescription to lose weight. The pills went in and the weight came off. She was now filling prescriptions from four different doctors; uppers, downers, painkillers, sleeping pills and diet pills. One afternoon while she was working at the restaurant, she started to hear voices buzzing in her head and became disoriented.

Rhonda noticed that she was kind of weaving around and asked, "Are you okay Dianne? You don't look so good, maybe you should lie down."

Dianne tried to answer but couldn't speak or focus on the face that was talking to her.

Rhonda grabbed her by the arm "I'm taking you to the hospital" she told her as she led her out to the car.

The doctor at the hospital emergency ward did a few tests and concluded that she had overdosed. She was now an official drug addict and the doctor convinced her that she needed to go to a detox program after discovering the number of drugs she was on. The doctor's office arranged it all for her to check in the following week for a twenty-eight day detox program and she never really thought much about it, just went along with it. Her mind was too muddled. She checked in with two huge suitcases and her own special pillow as if she was going on a luxury cruise or something.

At the detox centre they kept urging her to admit that she was an addict but she couldn't do it and never did admit that she was an addict of any sort throughout the whole twenty-eight days; she just needed some time off from her crazy life. At the end of the twenty-eight days, she took Alexander and went to Greece again. She felt good and looked good; better than she had in a very long time. Some of the fog in her mind had cleared as well as some of the chemicals from her body. Shortly after her arrival in Athens, she searched out Tomas and learned that he was married. She was devastated.

"I am so sorry, I made such a big mistake when I didn't marry you" she told him. You're the only man I've ever loved" she tearfully confessed to him.

He looked her in the eye and told her "I have a good wife" and walked away from her, ignoring her pitiful cries.

Devastated by Tomas' rejection, she plunged into a depression again and was back on the pills, all of them. This time though, she added cocktails. They spent three months in Athens, Dianne and her son, spending money like it was going out of style; partying at the best hotels, buying expensive jewelry, toys for Alexander, clothes, spa treatments, whatever took her fancy; whatever she thought might make her feel better.

Then Michael began calling and begging her to come back. "Let's start over again, I miss you and Alexander, please come home."

They went home to Montreal and Michael swore he and Rhonda were finished but Rhonda didn't see it that way. Rhonda would call the house and threaten to kill herself if Michael didn't come back to her. The reconciliation never happened; Michael went back to Rhonda and Dianne went back to bingo.

When the pills couldn't kill the pain anymore and the depression was worse than ever and she felt so utterly lost and alone, Dianne checked herself in for another detox session at the addictions treatment centre. It was different this time. This time she understood what they were talking about when they spoke of addictions and feelings, guilt and remorse. She wasn't there just so she would look better for her next trip to Greece; she was there to fix her insides, not her outsides, she had hit a bottom and she was ready. At the end of the detox, she went into a six-week rehab program. She was the only woman there most of the time and ended up cooking for everyone because no one else knew how to cook. She was so busy trying to control the entire place, making sure everything was clean and tidy, bossing people around, telling them what to do that she lost sight of what she was really there for.

The counselors put her to work out in the garden just to get her out of the kitchen where she was trying so hard to control everything. Gardening was something she had never even thought about doing before and she was not impressed. It was dirty work, her beautiful nails were ruined; she just didn't see the joy in it but did as she was told. If anything, it gave her a measure of solitude that she had never known before. Michael came to visit every Sunday while Dianne was in the treatment centre;

it was a long drive, about three hours each way. It really touched him that she was in this place. He just could not understand the depth of her problem because he felt he had no real addictions himself so could not relate. They talked and walked when he visited and decided that they would go back to the separate bedroom/same house arrangement when she came home and see how it went. She felt like she did love him in some bizarre way and that she needed him in her life.

Dianne got through the six weeks of treatment and came home with no fanfare; just went back to work the next morning at the restaurant as if nothing had changed; as if nothing had happened. Michael and Rhonda were still together even though no one acknowledged it. It became clear that there was nothing left of the marriage. Dianne rationalized that there was now nothing wrong with her having an affair here or there when she decided she needed a man's attention. The affairs never lasted and they never really meant much, but they helped her feel alive.

Dianne had been clean and sober for about a year now but had not been able to quit bingo. She would go to the bingo hall and buy everything she could get her hands on; all the scratch tickets and 50/50 draws and door prize draws and then find a chair in the darkest corner as far away from the others as possible. All by herself, she would sit there and bang down the dabbers on the flimsy paper cards. This had all seemed like so much fun before but now it just felt so lonely and sad and here she was, eyes brimming with tears trying to see through the blur to mark the cards.

One particularly crowded night, a woman came and put her cards down across the table from Dianne.

"Okay if I sit here?" the woman asked as she pulled out a chair. Dianne looked up

"Yeah, sure" she said as she tried to wipe her eyes without being too noticeable.

They played in silence for a while; Dianne's eyes drying as she focused on the cards.

At the break, sipping coffee out of paper cups, the woman asked Diane "Is everything okay, do you need anything?"

"No" Dianne sighed, "I'm just kind of depressed."

"Maybe it's all this!" the woman said, waving her arm around the room. Dianne looked at her, puzzled. "The bingo, the gambling" she said as she looked her straight in the eyes. "My friend was so addicted to bingo that she lost everything; her house, her car, everything! One day someone told her about Gamblers Anonymous and she got her life under control by going to the meetings. Maybe that's your problem. Maybe they can help you too."

Dianne just shook her head from side to side slowly, not wanting to look at the woman. "Uh, no, I don't think so, gambling is not a problem for me."

She was really insulted and angry that someone, a complete stranger, would say those things to her. She packed up her dabbers and left the bingo hall but all the way home she could not get the woman's words out of her head. Her friend had lost everything. That was how Dianne felt sometimes, like she would lose everything; that she was just on the verge of losing it all, including her mind.

The next morning she made up her mind to try it. She looked up the number for Gamblers Anonymous in the phone book and talked to someone on the other end who told her where the meetings were held. She went that night and experienced a brief feeling of release from her negative state of mind so she continued going to the meetings once a week and stayed away from the bingo halls. But this was not the cure-all that she was looking for either. The program emphasized honesty and she felt as though she was living a lie; still working with Michael at the restaurant pretending they were a couple while everyone knew they weren't really together; that Michael and Rhonda were in fact, a couple. It was unbearably humiliating for Dianne to have to face these people each and every day knowing that they knew.

There are many ways to deal with addictions and after doing some research, Dianne came to the conclusion that she had to deal with her drug addiction and signed up for a healing workshop; a three-day program where she would learn to release her anger and hopefully begin to feel better about herself. It was one of the hardest things she had ever done. They asked her to write about her feelings and she had never attempted to do that before. It was powerful; as though writing the words down on paper released their hold on her. But it wasn't all out yet. She went back for two more healing workshops over the next year and was devastated when she realized that in all of her writings she had not once included, not once even mentioned, her son, like he wasn't even part of her life. She suffered unbelievable guilt over this and learned that she had to go through a grieving process.

One of the questions she had to answer was "How did you show your partner love?"

Her answer was "I cooked and cleaned and laid out his clothes".

The counselor told her "That is not love; he could have paid someone to do that."

That is what Dianne thought love was, looking after someone like she looked after her father, then her husband. She worked hard on getting herself healthy and when she felt strong enough, she left Michael for good.

She told him "I don't want to live like this anymore and there is nothing you can say about it. I'm leaving."

Alexander stayed with his father and Dianne made a feeble attempt at remote parenting but knew now that she was exactly the kind of mother that her own mother had been, but still did not know how to change it.

Michael and Dianne finally divorced which enabled Michael and Rhonda to marry while Dianne went into one unhealthy relationship after another. Her first serious relationship ended in disaster; they met at a Gamblers Anonymous meeting, dated a while and decided to move in together. Dianne knew nothing of Sam's history of severe depression and not long after they had moved in together, found him dead in the garage with a bottle of whiskey between his legs, slumped over the steering wheel of his car with the motor running. She never knew that he was in so much pain that he would rather die than live. Now she would live with the guilt of Sam's death. Maybe she could have done something, but what? She told herself again and again that if he was that desperate to leave this world there was nothing she could have done.

Single again, knowing she had to stay away from anti-depressants and painkillers, Dianne tried Narcotics Anonymous meetings for a while, popping in and out of AA meetings and Gamblers Anonymous meetings. She felt that she just wasn't getting anything out of these programs though and went for more counseling and devoted the next few years to upgrading her psychology degree as she set her sights on working with abused children. Her life seemed to be a little more in control, a little more comfortable, when she met Dennis at one of the meetings she went to off and on. He seemed nice enough so they went out a few times and he told her he wanted a relationship with her. Soon enough, she found out that he was very, very controlling and Dianne felt compelled to agree with him on everything to avoid confrontation. She felt manipulated but still allowed him to move into her house hoping he would pay a share of the rent. He never paid her anything and they fought and argued all the time. He was like a bull in a china shop, always breaking things but never fixing them. He did not want anyone else at the house; especially not Dianne's family and she resented him for that, so after about six months she told him he had to leave. He left in a fit of fury and never came back.

Now it was time to heal. Dianne began doing inner child workshops to deal with the rage she felt toward her mother. She could never get past the feelings that went with the knowledge that her mother had tried to abort her and never really wanted her. She knew this was why she had never felt any connection to her mother but how could she live like this for the rest of her life?

She learned about the sexual abuse she suffered from an uncle at three years of age and also that her own father had abused her. There were many deep-rooted sexual problems to uncover. She had no trust of men; her father was not trustworthy and she ended up living with her husband exactly the way her mother had lived with her father. Her mother had been emotionally distant from her and she was emotionally distant from her own son. She learned that she was repeating the pattern of what had been done to her. She took her rage out on every relationship she ever had. She learned about the amends she needed to make to her son for the neglect, the verbal and emotional abuse and most of all, for not being there for him as a mother. She had to make financial amends for money she had stolen from Alexander's bank account to finance her years of gambling. It was both humiliating and embarrassing to admit this, not only to her son, but also to her ex-husband. She had to admit that she had always been jealous of Alexander, jealous that he got more attention from Michael than she did. Michael nurtured Alexander; showed him the love he needed and taught him how to love. They had a connection that Dianne never had with her son; never had with anyone.

When she got really honest with herself, she had to admit that she hadn't even wanted a child and deep down she knew that she had treated him horribly, always trying to demean him and anything he did. She made the amends, as painful and difficult as they were, and now knew that she had a right to be angry about the abuse she suffered. She had never loved herself; never felt that she was good enough and had made her family suffer for that. Her parents were both terribly wounded in their own right, but she couldn't feel any compassion for them until she mended her childhood with therapy and found out why she felt the way she did, emotionally and physically. The recovery groups were not enough to get Dianne to this point. It took a lot of therapy to heal the anger she was holding on to. She felt that the drugs, the gambling and the booze were to kill the pain and that she was never truly addicted to them. Those things were merely the symptoms of her pain. Dianne believed that her so-called addictions were not diseases but merely symptoms of her childhood issues of emotional abandonment and sexual abuse.

With a strong belief in God and utilizing a program of living, gone are the days when she prayed to God to give her cancer so that people would feel sorry for her and then they would know that it was their fault that she was dying of cancer. Gone are the days when she would sit locked in the bathroom scratching her thighs with a nail file till they bled when her husband would come home after spending the night with his lover. Gone are the days when she would ask God why he was punishing her. She now knew that God was not the same as her father, the ultimate controller, and she didn't have to prove anything to anyone, not even God. She was not being punished by anyone but herself. God gave her free will and there would be no more blaming. God loved her and she could trust that. She found out that it is easy enough to believe in a power greater than yourself but very hard to trust that same higher power when your earthly mother and father have broken the bond of trust.

It hasn't been an easy journey and Dianne still has to work the steps of the recovery programs and continue with her therapy to avoid sliding back into that verbally and emotionally abusive person. There are always issues that bring up newfound insecurity, jealousy or mistrust so the recovery is ongoing. Dianne lives alone now by choice and has a healthy, loving relationship with her son.

The End

# CHAPTER FOUR
# TERRINA

The baby was just five and a half pounds, gasping for air, her tiny lips blue. The mother was just a child herself, maybe fifteen. It was 1955 and pregnant teenagers were whisked out of town to go and "live with an aunt" not to return unless they were prepared to come back alone and keep the dirty secret for eternity. The nurses were all Sisters of the Order of St. Cecilia and did not have a lot of compassion for the young mother and her baby. She had been at the Home for Unwed Mothers for the last three months awaiting the birth of her baby and the moment the newborn's eyes imprinted into Bonnie's she knew she could never leave this baby. Knowing full well that if she stayed at the Home the baby would be taken away by the Nuns, she packed up the tiny bundle she named Terrina and fled. She headed for the General Hospital downtown, having overheard one of the other girls at the home say that a girl could go there for help if she was desperate and desperate she was.

As she walked through the entrance of the hospital, she spotted the Inquiries sign over a desk in the corner, approached the security guard and asked, "Is there someone here that can help me?"

The old man shook his head and snorted his disgust at this child with a baby and pointed a fat finger behind him at a door that said Family Services.

The young woman at the desk inside seemed pleasant and asked her to "Please have a seat till someone can see you".

Bonnie sat and waited, thankful that the baby slept contentedly. After what seemed like a long time, a tall, thin man with coke bottle spectacles came out and whispered something to the young woman at the Inquiries desk.

He then walked back through the door and the young woman at the desk said to Bonnie "You can go in now" as she tilted her head toward a sign on a door that read Director of Family Services. The man motioned for Bonnie to have a seat across from the desk where he sat and she began talking before she was sitting down, telling of her terrible plight; homeless with a hungry baby and nowhere to go and............. He held up his hand like a traffic cop to stop her, not looking up even once, all the while busily reading something and marking it up with a pencil. All of a sudden, he put down his pencil, ripped off a piece of paper from the pad he had been writing on and handed it to her. There was an address scribbled on it, and as she looked up, the Director of Family Services handed across the desk a small bound paper book, which he explained was a coupon book that she could redeem for groceries; enough to last her for one month.

As he peered at her through the thick glass circles, he told her in a condescending tone, "This is the best we can do for you. You've gotten yourself into a difficult situation but you can't expect us to fix it for you. This is the address of a boarding house where you can stay for one month and there are enough grocery coupons to tide you over until you can find work. I strongly suggest you find yourself a situation as a live-in housemaid or such and give the child up for adoption. Come back here when you're ready to hand over the child." The man stood up and held the door open for her to leave.

Bonnie looked down at the coupon book in her hand and wondered what she had expected them to do for her. Whatever it was, this wasn't it. She held Terrina close and practically ran out of the building.

The boarding house was a monstrous old rundown place right downtown just a short bus ride from the hospital so it wasn't hard to find and she didn't have much to carry besides the baby. All of the clothes and belongings they had between them fit into one small canvas bag. Bonnie showed the note to the large woman who opened the door after she rang the bell. Mrs. Weber was the landlady of the house and fully in charge. She looked at the note and took Bonnie over to a desk to sign her name in a register next to Room 4F.

"I'll put you in 4F up on the top floor so the baby won't disturb the other tenants you know" she puffed as they climbed up the four flights of stairs. By the time they got to the fourth floor, the landlady was completely out of breath and gasping as she pointed to the bathroom down the hall that was for the use of all the tenants on that floor; not a pretty sight. It was summer and 4F was stifling. Mrs. Weber banged on the paint encrusted window casing a few times and finally got it open wide enough to get a little fresh air moving, then left after showing Bonnie the list of rules on the back of the door. There was an old wardrobe closet with three wire hangers in it, a lumpy iron frame bed with some sheets waiting to be put on and a dresser with three big drawers in the stuffy room. Bonnie pulled a drawer from the dresser and lined it with the flat pillow off the bed to serve as a cradle for the baby and laid her in there with room to spare.

At first it was kind of fun to have this baby to play with; like a real live doll, but she demanded so much of her time, always crying and fussing and with no maternal guidance, Bonnie could never seem to figure out just what it was that Terrina needed. The food ration coupons hadn't lasted more than a week, so she got a job at the coffee shop two blocks away working split shifts. She would leave the baby alone in the room for two hours at a time for the breakfast and lunch rushes. Most of the time it seemed to work out okay and she didn't really worry about leaving the baby alone. It was only a couple of hours at a time; the baby sometimes slept longer than that she reasoned, but Bonnie would often lose track of time and be late getting back. The baby was beginning to suffer from the neglect. A surprise visit by a family service nurse while Bonnie was at work found the baby alone and hungry in the sweltering room during one of the lunch shifts. Terrina was taken away from Bonnie and her name entered into foster care.

Bonnie was devastated and repeatedly made promises to never leave Terrina alone again and would temporarily get the baby back until the next time she got caught. Family Services did not condone babies surviving on bread dipped in milk and sugar, which was practically all that Bonnie was feeding the baby now on her meager earnings. By the time Terrina turned 3 years old, she was removed from Bonnie's care for the last time. Bonnie would never see her child again.

Terrina's new life began when Howard and Elaine finalized her adoption and within a year adopted another child; a six-month old boy they named Jake. They grew up together as brother and sister.

By the time she was about ten years old, Terrina was already experiencing emotional problems. Even though she always did well in school, she was convinced that she was going to get a bad report card for the final term of grade six and was terrified of what her mother would do to her. It became such an obsession that she decided she could not bear the consequences of her potential failure and made the decision to end it all.

In the bathroom medicine cabinet, she found a package of Howard's razor blades. She carefully took the paper wrapping off one of the blades and put it flat into her open hand, walking slowly to her bedroom. She sat down on the bed, feeling cold and shaky and held the razor blade in her right hand between her thumb and forefinger but her hand was shaking so badly, she kept dropping the blade into the deep shag rug. Every time she bent down to pick it up, she thought she would throw up. By the third attempt to pick it out of the rug, she felt so dizzy she could hardly focus so she lay down on the bed, leaving the razor blade stuck in the rug, not sure what to do next.

Just then, she was jolted back from her thoughts by her mother screaming at her from the kitchen; "Terrina! Get downstairs and set the table for supper. Now!"

She couldn't go through with it. She wanted to die but not like this. She hung over the side of the bed and carefully picked the razor blade out of the rug. When she sat up, she felt nauseous again, ran to the bathroom and vomited till she was empty then checked herself in the mirror. Still alive; maybe next time.

When she got downstairs, her mother was angry. "What is the matter with you? You look terrible! Go and comb your hair!" Terrina went back upstairs feeling like a ghost. Maybe she really was dead and this was Hell, maybe nothing changes when you die. She pulled the comb through her hair and put it back up on the shelf before heading downstairs to set the table.

Terrina's relationship with her controlling mother was never easy. A few days after the razor blade incident, Terrina came home from school to find Elaine waiting for her at the front door and in her hand was Terrina's diary. Her precious, secret diary! She had been reading it! She had the book open at the page where Terrina had written about how she wanted to slash her wrists with her father's razor blades and she was furious.

Elaine shook the little pink book out in front of her and spit through clenched teeth "If anyone ever finds out about this stupid suicide plan of yours, they will take your little brother away from you and it will be all your fault!" "That's right" She screamed at Terrina "We will send him back and you will have to live with that for the rest of your life!"

After that, life became even more painful than before for Terrina until she made the decision that if she wanted to survive, she had to stop caring because caring just made her feel worse. If she just didn't care about anyone or anything she would feel better and the worst that could happen now would be that her mother would actually kill her, and then she'd be really dead and wouldn't have to worry about anything anymore.

Terrina did stop caring about what her mother said and started smoking cigarettes when the neighbors down the street offered them to her. They were bikers and she really liked them. They never yelled at her or called her stupid; they just let her hang around. They would leave her to babysit their houseful of kids till all hours and pay her fifty cents an hour and sometimes a joint of marijuana. The money was nice but the marijuana was what made it really worthwhile. A few tokes and everything looked so much better; she could laugh about the smallest things, just sit and smile and maybe even have a beer with the bikers if they came home drunk.

Terrina's adoptive father Howard was a loving, caring father but he wasn't home much, so when he was there, Elaine was very attentive, especially if he brought company. She loved to entertain; loved to impress people with little appetizers on the good plates and the fancy serviettes she kept for just those occasions. Howard would mix drinks and she would flit around the room in all her glory swirling her dress behind her. Terrina liked these party nights because she could get away with so much more when her mother was preoccupied. By now, at sixteen years old, Terrina partied every chance she got. Partying meant getting drunk and Terrina would drink anything for a buzz. She absolutely loved how she felt when she drank; it was the only time she really felt good and she started to feel the need to get to that high more and more all the time.

Terrina fantasized about leaving home constantly. Bonnie was getting harder on her about her schoolwork and Terrina couldn't take it anymore, so she stopped bringing homework home. That way she didn't have to deal with her mother making her do it over and over again until it was absolutely perfect. She would demand to see every scrap of paper, every assignment, every book that she brought into the house; they would be scrutinized and criticized; nothing was ever quite right.

"Do it over again and do it right this time!" she would yell in Terrina's face while she pinched her arm. "I better not be getting any phone calls from the school that your work isn't good enough! We brought you up better than that!" If any of Terrina's friends came over to the house, Elaine would interrogate and embarrass them with personal questions or quiz them about their parents and if Terrina objected, Elaine would start yelling and swearing at Terrina right in front of them. The last time she ever invited her friends over was the day Elaine slapped her across the face in front of them. The girls were so embarrassed for Terrina, they all left. After that day, Terrina and her mother did not speak to each other unless it was to fight.

It was after a screaming match that got out of control that Terrina left home. She had skipped school that Friday afternoon to go and smoke up at a friend's house and the school called her mother to report her absence. The instant she walked in the door at her usual coming-home-from-school time Elaine pounced. She grabbed Terrina by the arm and flung her down into a chair in the corner of the kitchen where she could tower over her.

"What the Hell is the matter with you? Do you think I'm so stupid that I don't know what you're up to? The people who run the school respect me. Nobody respects you. They tell me when you don't show up at school. Did you hear me? Nobody respects you! You are such a useless waste of time!"

Terrina lifted herself up off the chair, pushing against her mother, but Elaine pushed back and Terrina landed on the floor. This just infuriated Elaine even more and she bent down to yank her daughter back up on to the chair. As she made a lunge for Terrina, she knocked the cutting board off the table and the bread knife clanged to the floor right beside Terrina. Elaine's rage had total control of her now as she scooped up the knife while Terrina was scrambling up off the floor. Terrina was going to make a run for it. She had seen the knife hit the floor and was afraid of what she might do if she got hold of it. She was so terrified she was numb; she couldn't remember how to stand up.

Not prepared to lose the battle, Elaine made a grab for Terrina, this time with the hand holding the knife. The tip of the knife went into Terrina's back just above her right shoulder blade. Elaine stopped in her tracks with the knife still in her hand. A circle of blood started to form on the pink t-shirt. She stood there perfectly still as Terrina turned around and looked straight into her mother's eyes. One big tear rolled down Terrina's cheek as she got up and walked slowly out of the kitchen. There was no time to stop and think about what had just happened. She had to leave this place. She could not trust herself to live in the same house with her mother any longer. The last thing she wanted was to be like her mother, and if she stayed, she would have to fight back.

Terrina went to her room and threw some clothes into her backpack, grabbed her accordion and left. Elaine was still standing in the kitchen trying to sort out in her head what had just happened. She had to get her mind around the facts to reassure herself that she had done nothing wrong. Her head was swimming so she sat down and tried to compose herself. It didn't take long for her to confirm that she was not to blame for anything. "That child is impossible" she thought to herself as she started to straighten out the mess. It would be a long time before they would even see each other again.

Terrina moved in with her grandmother on the condition that she stay in school and get a part-time job. For the next year, Terrina went faithfully to classes and worked weekends at the East Island Amusement Park. During the summer, it was a great job working outside selling tickets or hot dogs and cotton candy. It seemed as though things might be okay now. The last day of the season the stalls were all shuttered up and the whole crew was treated to a bit of a party with pizza and cokes. Terrina was really enjoying herself; she had made friends and it felt good. Before she knew it, almost everyone had left and there was only one more ferry back to the mainland for the night so the last little group of stragglers headed over toward the dock. She decided she had better go to the bathroom before she got on the ferry and ducked inside the ladies washroom on the midway.

Just as she was coming out of the stall, she heard the outside door slam. "Jody, is that you?" No answer. "Jody, quit fooling around, I'll be right out!" Just as she turned from the sink to dry her hands she saw something move out of the corner of her eye and could hear someone breathing. She started to turn around and was knocked to the floor, hitting her head on the porcelain sink as she fell to the ground. The world starting spinning and everything went black. She must have been unconscious for just seconds because when she opened her eyes, she screamed at the sight of the reeking man sprawled on top of her. He was trying to pull down her shorts with such force that she was bouncing off the concrete floor. Her screams reached the others who came running as fast as they could. Bradley had picked up a board on the way and wasted no time smashing it down on the pervert's back. That got an instant reaction. He rolled off Terrina and moaned as Bradley took the opportunity to smash the board down on his head. He was out. Terrina struggled to her feet and got outside. Jody and Bradley insisted she needed to go to the hospital or call the cops.

"No, let's just leave. Now!" she pleaded. Seeing how upset she was and not wanting to push it, they all headed back to the dock and caught the last ferry to the mainland within minutes; the last ferry that would run till the next day. Terrina hoped the pervert would lay there and die. No one spoke on the way back. The next day she packed up her knapsack and headed downtown. To Hell with school. No goodbyes, no explanations. She was 16 years old and didn't need anybody. Her grandmother would worry but that was her problem.

It was easy to get a job as a waitress in the city and she made pretty good tips. The staff was allowed to eat one meal a day at no charge so that helped. She moved in with one of the other waitresses who had a furnished apartment right downtown; a seedy little place but the price was right. They worked the afternoon shift from noon till about eight or nine o'clock, depending on how busy it was. Then the night could begin, off with the drab uniform and on with the mini skirts, platform shoes and lots of makeup. She felt so glamorous.

The legal drinking age was twenty-one and Terrina was still only sixteen but had a bunch of phony ID cards that said she was anywhere from twenty-one to twenty-seven. The bouncers at the bars didn't care who you really were or how old your ID said you were, as long as you had it. The people who worked and drank at these bars were not exactly the city's finest; most of them were probably not who they said they were. What they had in common was that they all agreed the answer to everything could be swallowed, inhaled or injected. It was so easy here.

After a few beers at the bar one night, Terrina and three of her friends decided to take a taxi over to a house where they could get some really good hash. It wasn't actually that far to walk, but they didn't want to waste a beer buzz so they piled into a taxi and started counting out their money as the driver pulled out into the traffic. The light ahead was green as they drove through the intersection. The other car came through the red light and smashed into the taxi's passenger side pushing it into the car beside it, pinning it between the two cars. The sound had been like a bomb going off. Suddenly there were lights and sirens everywhere. An ambulance took Terrina and one of the other girls to the hospital while the paramedics patched up the other two girls and the driver. Terrina had been sitting where the worst impact had been and was in bad shape. Her right leg was completely crushed and her face had been cut in so many places it would take a hundred and fifty stitches to close it up. The car that hit them was carrying five people; all drunk including the driver; miraculously none seriously injured.

For the next year and a half she lived back at home with her parents. They were patient with her while she went through three plastic surgeries to restore her face, countless surgeries to rebuild her leg and painful physiotherapy to teach her to walk again. Terrina stayed away from drugs and alcohol during the whole year and a half that she was recovering. When she was finally all healed up and mobile, she found another waitress job; new friends, new parties, and started staying out late at night, sometimes not sleeping at all. Partying was still where it was at for Terrina, but her mother laid down the law and told her that she wasn't going to put up with any of her bad behavior again. Threats meant little or nothing to Terrina. She had stopped caring long ago and had no intention of ever coming home right after work, no matter where she lived; it was time to move on anyway. The very next time she stayed out all night, she found her bags on the front lawn when she came home in the morning.

"Who needs them anyway" she thought as she dragged her bags down the street. "I'll call Dirk." Dirk was a guy that she had been partying with for the past few weeks and he had a car, an old station wagon which he basically lived in. Dirk was a kind hearted drunk; a few years older than Terrina but he always told her that he loved her, even the times when she didn't want to have sex with him, a trait she found very endearing. He was at his usual table at the usual bar and when she told him about her predicament, he lost no time in offering her the spacious comfort of his home on wheels for as long as she liked. She was thrilled; problem solved.

Living in a car seemed perfectly acceptable at the time. They rarely retired for the night until they were completely blitzed and they could mooch off some friends with an apartment for a hot shower now and then; what else did they need, they had each other. Somehow, the crazier things were for Terrina, the more normal they seemed. After a few weeks of this blissful blur of togetherness they decided they should get married. They both had jobs of a sort and between the two of them they made enough money to pay rent on a tiny furnished apartment downtown, but after the booze and the drugs, there wasn't much left and the marriage lasted only ten months. It never got nasty or violent, but they soon came to realize that they didn't actually like each other all that much, so it was easy to agree to end it. Dirk moved out of their little apartment back into his car and Terrina began the next chapter of her life.

By now, Terrina had started to favor the high from certain chemicals over booze and was found unconscious one morning by some of her druggie friends. They had come by to see if she was home and found her sprawled half on, half off the threadbare couch that served as her bed. She looked bad and they tried all the tricks they knew to see if she was okay but nothing seemed to rouse her. They waited a while and when nothing changed, they called an ambulance. This time there were no stitches or broken bones. She was treated with prescription drugs as a psychiatric patient. They let her out after ten weeks and she couldn't wait to have a drink. She had had enough drugs for a while.

Things soon went back to the way they were, working at the restaurant, getting involved with one loser after another and drinking away the pain and the loneliness. Every relationship seemed to start out okay but they always plunged into abuse so she would move on. Then she met Allan; Big Al, his friends called him. Big Al was as nice as could be sober, but that wasn't often. They had been living together for six months with things getting worse all the time when Terrina found herself pregnant. This did not improve Big Al's mood much. He blamed her for the pregnancy.

"How in the Hell could you be so stupid? I don't want no kid!" They fought about the baby constantly and she begged Al to stop blaming her. She did her best to hide the black eyes and bruises and managed to make it through the pregnancy in one piece and delivered a perfectly healthy baby girl. The baby was so perfect, a miracle, a little girl who looked just like a little mini Terrina. Worried about the safety of the tiny baby she named Leah she tried to avoid Al as much as she could, but she had not moved out of the apartment yet. He slapped her around every time he drank but still she stayed; her mind so muddled that it never really occurred to her that she had a choice; that she could leave before it was too late and then that day came.

Terrina picked up Leah from the babysitter after her shift at the restaurant and headed for the apartment secure in the knowledge that Al would not be home from work till midnight. After she unbundled the baby, she carried her into the kitchen to make them both some supper. She turned on the radio and danced with the baby in her arms, happy to be alone with her little girl while she made some supper. Soon after they had eaten, the baby was getting sleepy so she got her ready for bed and put her in the crib, singing to her softly. Terrina had just sat down to watch TV when Al burst into the apartment. He was drunk and he was mad. He had been fired from his job and she was going to pay for it.

He walked over to where she was sitting on the couch and screamed in her face "You fucking bitch! It's all your fault, you and that brat of yours!"

Al had never acknowledged that he was the father of the baby even though there was never any doubt that he was, so it was always her brat.

"You'll pay for this!" he screamed as his open hand came down across her face so hard she heard her neck snap.

He picked her up by one arm and slammed her into the wall. As she slid down the wall she pleaded with him "Please, please, don't hurt the baby" but he didn't hear her. His drunken fury deafened him as he flopped down on the couch, in front of the TV with what was left of a bottle of whiskey.

Every time she managed to crawl to her feet to try and get to the bedroom to get the baby and get out of there, he would get madder and madder and the beating continued all through the night. When she begged him to stop, he smashed her face into the radiator and when she tried to move he stomped on her feet with his huge steel toed work boots. He grabbed her by the hair and jerked her head back so many times that her neck began to swell. Her body was battered and bruised beyond belief and by the end of the night, the room looked as though a tornado had been through it. She had been flung around the room like a rag doll over and over and over. Everything was either broken or had her blood on it.

Finally, he left and Terrina tried to crawl over to the phone to call the police. With the effort of raising her head she passed out and lay unconscious for another hour. The next time she came to, she heard the baby crying and that was all she needed to summon the strength to get up. The baby had somehow slept through the entire night but must have been crying for a while because when Terrina got to the crib she was flushed and gasping for air. Terrina crawled into the kitchen to get Leah a bottle of milk out of the fridge, crawled back to the bedroom, pulled the side of the crib down and sat there on the floor feeding the hungry baby. Her mind was swirling. She had to get out of there before he came back. She finished feeding the baby and sat her on the floor while she limped carefully and painfully to the bathroom and swallowed all the painkillers she could find. Then she threw some of the baby's stuff into a bag and called a cab.

The cab dropped them off at the nearest hospital emergency where a nurse put her in an examining room as soon as she walked in. The doctor was horrified at her condition and convinced her that she could have been killed and under no circumstance should she return to that apartment. The nurses looked after the baby while they patched up all the cuts and bruises and put a cast on her left wrist after the x-ray revealed that it was cracked in three places. The nurses were amazed that she had actually made it to the hospital in the shape she was in considering the amount of blood she had lost. They kept Terrina and Leah for twenty-four hours observation and then discharged her on the condition that someone pick them up. She took the doctor's advice about not returning to the apartment and called a friend who said her and Leah could come and stay there for a while. She couldn't call her parents, they had not spoken for several years and she had heard that her mother was dying of cancer so they probably had enough to worry about already.

Terrina recovered and life goes on, as it has a way of doing, and once she got her strength back, she went back to work part-time evenings and took the upgrading courses she needed to enroll in university. Going to school and working with a small child at home required a lot of extra energy which she did not have, but managed to get by taking amphetamines to get her through to graduation.

Once she got her degree, Terrina got a good job where she met and married Phil, a man who was not abusive in the ordinary sense but extremely neglectful which she ignored for the most part because, in her experience, this was the best she had done so far. They managed to have a son together which made the whole arrangement seem worthwhile. Life began to feel almost comfortable or normal even though Phil was distant and didn't really care much about her or anything she cared about. They drank together but not in the crazy ways of her past; they were civilized drinkers with a nice home to drink in. Terrina continued working days and furthering her education with night classes and they stayed married for more than ten years.

In that tenth year, Terrina consciously decided to allow herself to feel, for the first time, all those experiences that she had locked away in her mind since her childhood. It felt safe now and she thought maybe she could deal with those feelings but she was wrong. It was too much for her and the stress and anxiety of trying to come to terms with the memories resulted in a total breakdown. She lost her job, her husband had an affair, which he did nothing to hide, and she spent months in the hospital psychiatric ward when she began having seizures.

Phil had no use for a sick wife and proceeded to clean out her bank accounts and move his girlfriend into their house while she was still in the hospital. By the time she came home, he had turned both of her kids entirely against her, telling them all kinds of lies about her and had given away most of her belongings. With the help of a lawyer, she fought and managed to get them all out of the house because it was in her name, and he was forced to leave with the girlfriend. The kids left with him, still believing his lies about their mother.

Now she was alone with her pain in an empty house. The doctors had been adamant that she never, ever drink alcohol again. The seizures would become uncontrollable if she drank. She managed to stay sober for six months but any attempt to leave the house would cause her unbelievable anxiety. She was having a hard time functioning and at times, could hardly speak, so her doctor put her on an anti-anxiety drug with a warning that alcohol could not be taken with this drug; one drink would be like five. In desperation, Terrina rationalized that this could work; she would have one drink just so she could leave the house. She reasoned that she could take the drug along with the alcohol as long as she made sure that she if she went somewhere, there would be someone with her that would know what to do when she had a seizure. This was the only way she could leave the house; the rest of the time when she stayed home, she could drink as much as she needed and not worry about the seizures; no one would see her anyway. The seizures did not scare her at all.

This system worked for over a year until she grew tired of the worsened depression the alcohol brought on. She decided the booze had to go and she attempted to quit drinking many times over the next few years using every trick she could think of. Nothing worked. She was seeing a counselor; but nothing he said seemed to make any sense either. She went on tolerating her life at times and attempting to end it a few more times; usually intentional overdoses when the pain of the loneliness was too much to bear. She always felt very confused when she would wake up from yet another suicide attempt. Why couldn't she die when she wanted to? Maybe it was still the same Hell from her first attempt at ending it all when she was just a kid. Finally, she arrived at a seemingly workable combination of tranquilizers and alcohol that kept her going through the motions of life, albeit in some sort of hazy fog.

It was during this time that she started attending night classes once again to upgrade her skills so she could get back to work when she met Wilf. The most incredible thing about Wilf was that he didn't drink. Terrina always noticed who drank and who didn't and how much and how often, always comparing. She had never known anyone quite like him; she thought he was fascinating. The day after they attended a school function where Terrina had gotten drunk, Wilf took her aside and explained that the reason he didn't drink was that he was a recovering alcoholic. He told her how he had lost everything in his life because of his drinking, but had a new sober life now. He told her that she could make a choice just as he had, and that she could choose the path her life would take. The notion of making choices in her life had never occurred to Terrina. Life just happened and she had dealt with it as best she could. Five years of counseling had taught her that she needed to be more empowered in her own life, but the depression usually overshadowed everything and the more depressed she got, the more she drank and the cycle continued.

The idea of choosing a path for herself really appealed to Terrina and she went to an Alcoholics Anonymous open speaker meeting with Wilf the next night. Through all the years of drinking and drugging, it had never felt like an obsession, just a necessity, so when they talked about how unmanageable their lives had been and how powerless they were to change, she could not relate. Unmanageable was everyone else's fault but powerless was a weakness. She did not see herself as weak; not in any way; she was a survivor. But as the speaker told her story, Terrina was amazed at the similarities to her own life and for the first time ever, felt hopeful. She wanted to feel good like that speaker said she did. At the next meeting Wilf took her to, she felt lighter, almost high with the expectation of what was to come. She was a little nervous walking in to the meeting but Wilf held her arm as they descended the stairs into the church hall and when she saw the people there she was okay. They were people, just like her, more like her than anyone else in fact, and they welcomed her. They advised her to go to a meeting every day for ninety days and if she wanted her misery back after that, she could have it.

The twelve steps were presented as the program of recovery and she did them one by one, weeks turning into months, learning about herself along the way. Learning to deal with the hurt and pain of her past and sharing the experience and sadness with others lightened the heavy baggage that she had been carrying around every day of her life. There were new ways to handle people, places and things; new coping mechanisms and lots of positive change happening.

After her first year of sobriety, Terrina and Wilf were married and for the first time in her life she didn't have that empty feeling of being alone. These people were her family now; these recovering alcoholics that she had built meaningful, loving friendships with. Terrina learned to take care of herself and in turn, attracted people who were caring.

They say if you want to know who you are, look at your friends and you will know.

The End

# CHAPTER FIVE
# JOY

The headline on the Cornwall Daily Dispatch read "Cornwall Dolphins Champions" and directly beneath the headline was a large photo showing the Dolphins Swim Team lifting up a small girl peeking out from behind a big, shiny trophy. The article went on to say that Joy Parker, at the tender age of six, had taken the place of one of the regular team members when she fell ill and had helped to secure their victory in the final heat of the weekend swim meet. It hadn't taken much convincing from the coach for Joy to jump in to help out her older sister's team. Joy had been taking swimming lessons as long as she could remember, a natural born swimmer. She loved the water and had absolutely no fear associated with it so she was ecstatic to be in the race and when the whistle blew she swam as fast as she could without hesitation.

That was how Joy became famous. The people of Cornwall talked about that race and how Joy saved the day for a long time afterwards. At the tender age of six she had become an instant over-achiever; forever programmed to seek out praise and accolades to recreate that moment of glory.

Home was not a particularly fun place for Joy and her sister Sharon. Their father Martin was a mechanic who worked long hours and expected everything to be exactly the way he wanted when he came home after a long day at the garage. His days were long and he often worked seven days a week so when he was home, he was usually miserable, if not drunk and argumentative. After a grueling day at the garage, he always deserved a few beers at the local watering hole where all the hard working men gathered after work to unwind. The trouble was that it usually wound him up more than down, and he would head home with a bad attitude and take it out on the family.

It was the same thing every day. Martin would walk in the door and yell "Noreen, what's for supper?"

Noreen would drop whatever she was doing and run back to the kitchen to take his plate of food out of the oven where it had been placed to keep warm until he showed up. She would put it on the table in front of him and he would grunt something and dig in. Once he was done devouring whatever it was that she had placed in front of him, he headed for the lazy boy chair in front of the television with a bottle of beer and the newspaper. He would set the bottle of beer on the folding TV tray beside the chair and sit down, push the seat back and flip up the footrest before opening up the newspaper.

Noreen and the girls always kept their fingers crossed that he would turn on the television and watch the news or maybe even a hockey game so that he would be distracted enough not to focus on any noise they might be making. As long as no one bothered him or made any noise whatsoever, the evening could go well but if anybody disturbed him and HIS time, things would go bad quickly. If the kids went in and out of the back door one too many times or if Noreen talked on the phone in the kitchen too long, he would yell some expletive from the chair ordering them to stop doing whatever they were doing to ruin his time! And if the annoyance continued, he would have to get out of his chair and then there would be trouble. The danger level depended on how drunk he was; the drunker the meaner, and mean meant that he would come out swinging. The kids knew to make a run for it to avoid being hit and that would anger him even more. Noreen was usually the one who got the brunt of his anger though because she would be the only one left in sight. He liked to grab her by the arm and if she tried to defend herself, he would squeeze her arm hard and threaten her with a beating if she didn't shut up. She forever had bruises discoloring her upper arms and was never, ever seen wearing anything sleeveless, no matter how hot the weather got because if anybody saw those bruises, she wouldn't know how to explain them away. She knew how suspicious the finger mark bruises looked and made sure that no one; not even the kids, ever saw them.

School became an escape from home for the girls, especially for Joy, the over-achiever, who did well in school and spent as much time as she could there. The less time she had to spend at home, the better. There were lots of after-school teams and clubs to join and she joined them all at one time or another and everything she did, she did well.

By the time her parents divorced when she was about ten years old, she was well entrenched in the sports world of the school; often being voted captain of whatever team she was on at the moment; she was a great little athlete and everybody liked her. Her mother quickly adapted to the singles world and began dating and enjoying life as she had not done since before her marriage to Martin. Joy and Sharon didn't like Noreen dating much but kept it to themselves as long as Noreen left them alone to do what they wanted.

The first time Noreen left the girls alone for a weekend, Joy invited a bunch of her friends over to her house for a party. They carefully took the big punch bowl from the china cabinet and mixed up whatever liquor they could find with some ginger ale and maraschino cherries. They scooped up the punch into the little glass cups that were hanging on the edge of the punch bowl and all sat down on the living room floor to listen to Tommy James and the Shondelles on the record player. It wasn't long before everyone was up dancing and laughing; having a great time.

Joy woke up on the floor at about 4:00 a.m. Everyone was gone; she was all by herself. The nearly empty punch bowl was sitting in the middle of the floor in a big sticky mess. There were soggy potato chips mashed in to the green shag carpet. The record player was still playing; the needle was stuck and it was belting out something unintelligible over and over. Joy stood up and walked over to turn the record player off, being careful not to step on any of the little glass cups scattered around the floor. She couldn't understand what had happened. The last thing she remembered was having such a great time dancing and laughing, drinking the punch and eating chips. What happened to everybody? They were supposed to stay over for a slumber party and it wasn't even morning yet. She decided it was all too confusing to figure it out right now as tired as she was, flung herself down on the couch and fell asleep.

Even though Sharon was supposed to have stayed home to keep an eye on Joy for the weekend she had spent the night with her boyfriend so when she came home and found Joy asleep on the couch in the middle of the mess she was furious. If their mother found out, they would both be grounded. She yelled at Joy to wake up as she shook her shoulders; it was already almost noon and their mother would be home sometime in the afternoon.

"Get up Joy! We have to clean up this mess before Mom gets home! What were you guys doing last night? What a mess! You are going to be in so much trouble if she finds out you drank her booze!" She hesitated, "Wait, I know, we can fill up the bottles with water and she won't notice there's any missing. Hurry up and start picking up these chips and get a wet cloth" she ordered.

Joy followed the orders as they were issued; her head hurt and she didn't have the strength to argue. They managed to get the living room back in shape before their mother arrived home and if she noticed anything, she didn't mention it. Later that day, Joy tracked down some of the girls who had been at her slumber party to find out why they had left. One of the girls' mothers had found out that they were there without supervision and had dragged them all out, leaving Joy alone with the punch. She laughed about it, pretended she remembered everything and left it at that.

Joy had it all by the time she started high school; honor student, star athlete, and as a bonus she had blossomed into a beauty. Her brains and abilities had always gotten her a lot of attention and now she was getting the attention of boys too. She quickly caught on to the stir she created in them and learned to use it to satisfy her need for approval and recognition. They would tell her whatever she needed to hear to get what they wanted and she was okay with that. She went to a lot of parties and met a lot of guys but Darren was probably the best looking guy in the entire school and he just happened to be the quarterback of the football team. When he asked her out, she thought he could probably hear her heart pounding as she said "Yeah, sure, when?" trying to act nonchalant.

"There's a party at my brother's place tomorrow night."

"Yeah, okay, here's my address" she said without looking up as she scribbled the address down on a scrap of paper she tore from the corner of her notebook. She could hardly believe it, but it was destiny that they would become a couple; the two best looking, most popular, accomplished athletes in the school.

Darren liked to party as much as Joy did and between the two of them they could easily polish off a dozen beer. They didn't actually get along all that well, but they both craved the attention they got as the perfect couple so they both put up with a lot. They cheated on each other all the time, he with the cheerleaders and she with whoever could impress her with the most flattery. The attention of one male was definitely not enough for Joy and she slept with anyone she fancied without remorse. The sex was never sober though. She was always more or less drunk by the time they got around to the sex and every party was an occasion to get drunk for Joy. She would always drink till she was totally inebriated or passed out.

In spite of her excessive socializing, Joy still managed to excel in sports and was on the scouts lists in her senior year of high school. In the spring of her last year, she received a scholarship offer from a college in Arizona. She was thrilled and spent the next three months planning and packing, un-packing and re-packing. Small town girl makes it to the big time! She could just see the headline of the Cornwall Daily Dispatch with a picture of little Joy all grown up headed for the big time and any notion that she should slow down her drinking now that she was destined to be a professional athlete never crossed her mind and she continued to party it up for the rest of grade twelve.

Joy was a typical addict doing everything to the extreme whether it was studying, drinking or sports; it was all the same. Everything was an addiction, some healthy, some deadly, no difference to her, extreme was her normal. The night before she was to leave for college in Arizona, her friends held a farewell bush party in her honor with dozens of kids and enough beer to drown them all. They had a huge bonfire roaring and sticks sharpened up to roast wieners and marshmallows. Darren was being especially attentive on this, their last night together, and suddenly Joy was afraid; afraid to leave all this; her comfort zone, her drinking buddies; how could she ever fit in anywhere else, this was all she had ever known and she was a star here.

The plane left with one empty seat the next day. Joy spent the day alone in her bedroom nursing a vicious hangover, trying to avoid her mother.

Noreen was furious "How can you just NOT GO? What in God's name is wrong with you, you are missing out on your one chance of a lifetime! You will never get another chance like this if you screw this up! I swear you're ruining your life!" she yelled into Joy's bedroom door.

Everyone else seemed to be more disappointed than Joy that she didn't go, and suddenly, just like that, she wasn't a star anymore. Everything changed.

Joy decided to enroll in a carpentry course at a technical college in Hamilton because life in Cornwall was not the same anymore. Everyone was so disappointed in her that she couldn't stand it. She left Darren behind; he didn't seem to care, and plunged herself into the carpentry course where she got paired up with a guy called Mick on a few school projects. When he asked her out for a coffee after class, she jumped at it. She was desperately in need of attention, even though she would much rather have gone for a beer. It only took a few weeks before she discovered she was falling in love with Mick. She had never felt like this about anyone before. It was an all-consuming passion that made her heart lurch and her palms sweat; she couldn't stop thinking about him when he wasn't around; couldn't concentrate on anything; couldn't eat, couldn't sleep. When he confessed that he too was falling in love, she felt happier than she had since before she tossed the scholarship.

They had a great relationship. He was a very patient, understanding guy who put up with her drinking without complaint. He didn't drink much himself but was so enamored with Joy that it didn't seem to matter what she did. They moved in to a little apartment near the college and lived on love as much as they could and were really happy in their own little world until the next winter when Mick caught a flu that just wouldn't go away.

As the winter wore on, the flu symptoms persisted and became worse. Mick started to lose weight, becoming pale and weak, tiring easily; at night he would alternate a fever with chills, sweating up the sheets. When Joy noticed some tiny red spots under his skin, she convinced him to see a doctor. He went to the appointment and the doctor took all the routine tests and readings and told him that they would call him if there was anything to discuss. Ten days later, on his twentieth birthday, Mick received a call from the doctor's office asking him to come in to see the doctor that afternoon at 1:00 p.m.

They were worried before but now they were terrified. Mick and Joy showed up at the doctor's office as directed and were seated facing the doctor who was holding a sheaf of paper taken out of a file folder. He looked up and solemnly told them "I'm afraid it's not good news Mick. It's acute Lymphocyte Leukemia." After he let that sink in for a few seconds, the doctor came around to the front of the desk and put his hand on Mick's shoulder. Mick was staring ahead of him at nothing. The tears had started to well up in Joy's eyes but she was trying hard to listen to the doctor. The word leukemia was loud in her head as the doctor was going on and on, explaining exactly what acute Lymphocyte Leukemia was until Mick looked up at the doctor and asked "Am I going to die?"

The doctor carefully replied "We will definitely do everything we can to see that you don't Mick", but over the next few months, Mick got progressively worse, in and out of the hospital; all life had essentially stopped for him. Joy couldn't handle it. The worse he got, the more she drank. He died in the hospital six months after the diagnosis with his family by his side. Joy wasn't there; she was gone; she had run away; abandoned her first true love at his darkest hour.

The shame and guilt of what she had done; of not being there for Mick when he died was too much for her and she climbed into a bottle and stayed there for two weeks, not seeing anyone or leaving the apartment except to get more booze. When she was too late for the liquor store one night, she lost control and started banging on the windows, screaming obscenities at the empty store, but it wasn't empty. An employee inside called the police who showed up and threw her into a squad car to calm down. She quickly snapped out of it and assured the officers that she really meant no harm and would not cause any more trouble. They gave her a warning and told her to go straight home. She walked back to her empty apartment and stood at the door, key in hand feeling utterly lost and hopeless without her crutch, wondering what she was supposed to do now.

When she got inside she called her Uncle Dave who she knew had been a notorious drunk just like her dad, but had been sober for a long time now, and she knew she had to talk to someone about her drinking. Uncle Dave was glad to hear from her and assured her that everything would be okay; he would make a couple of phone calls and have someone come over and talk to her. About an hour later, the buzzer rang and she pressed the button to see who it was.

"Hi Joy, your Uncle Dave called us. Can we come in?"

Joy pressed the buzzer that would let them in. She opened the door and stood back not knowing what to expect. A minute later, two young women in their late twenties stood in the doorway. The taller one said "Hi, I'm Darcy and this is Shannon. Your Uncle Dave said you needed someone to talk to."

"Uh, yeah, I do, come in."

The one called Darcy did most of the talking; telling Joy all about how she had been such a hopeless drunk and how everything was so great now, but it was getting really late and Joy had a huge headache so she told them she needed to get some sleep. They came back the next night and took her to an AA meeting but Joy still had the headache and fidgeted uncomfortably throughout the meeting. "I'm not like these people!" she kept thinking. "I'm better than this, I can beat this so-called stupid disease myself". After the meeting she thanked the girls for the ride but knew she would not see them again. She wanted no part of their world. She was nineteen years old, way too young to worry about anything like that.

Nothing changed much over the next couple of years, in and out of relationships, her dependence on alcohol increasing all the time. She didn't care about much of anything at all anymore but managed to graduate from the carpentry course and got a job cabinet making.

It was common knowledge that the owner of the company she was working for was married, but that didn't stop her from accepting his invitation for drinks after work one night. That one night turned into most nights and his wife soon found out about the affair and kicked him out of their home. Bill was 46 years old with two teenage children but Joy didn't care; he was someone to drink with. His wife hired a good lawyer and took him for everything he had, so they ended up living in a cockroach-infested apartment where things went from bad to worse. Bill was not good at being poor and they fought continuously.

One bleary eyed morning, Joy looked apprehensively into her reflection in the mirror and really saw, for the first time, what she had become. She sat down on the toilet and stared at the pink plastic tiles on the wall, her mind going into overdrive. Something had to change and change now, before it was too late. As if in a dream watching herself, she moved through the apartment getting dressed, throwing a spare set of clothes into the knapsack she kept hanging on the back of the bedroom door; toothbrush, hairbrush, her little blue purse, her address book, filling up the bag thinking maybe those two women her Uncle Dave had sent over had it right after all. Just as she was about to go out the door she decided to leave a note for Bill then changed her mind, she didn't want anyone to know where she was going, especially Bill. He might do something stupid like try and break her out. Suddenly she was wide-awake and headed out the door.

She had looked up the address for a detox centre downtown that she had heard about and decided to blow part of her last twenty bucks on a cab to get there.

When she told the receptionist at the front desk that she wanted to check in she was told "Oh no, you have to be referred by your doctor ahead of time; you can't just walk in!"

This was all too much; she started to cry and couldn't stop. The receptionist called for some help and a counselor came out and calmed Joy down to the point where she could talk. He could see the distress she was in and told her that everything would be okay, that he could admit her for the seven day intake program; that there was someone leaving the following morning so there would be a spot.

She nodded her head in agreement and relaxed a little. She was really frightened of what she might do if she left here now. If they didn't help her, what would happen. He told her to just wait there while he went to get some forms to fill out. She waited and while he was gone, she blew her nose a few times and tried to calm down before he came back with the forms for her to sign.

Joy learned more about herself in that seven days than she ever thought possible and too soon the day came that she was to leave and now, more than ever, she was scared of herself and what she might do. They told her to go to lots of AA meetings, not to isolate herself and to phone someone if she had the urge to drink. She went back to the apartment because she had nowhere else to go. What a mess she had made of her life; all she had was what she could carry; no job; no future. Bill wasn't there; it looked as though he had cleared out while she was gone, but she wasn't even curious about where he might have gone; didn't care; just as well anyway, how could she stay sober with him around? There were a few cans of soup and beans left in the kitchen cupboard so she heated up the beans and sat on the bed eating them slowly as she tried to figure out what to do next.

She had the list of AA meetings in her knapsack and pulled it out as she carefully ate the beans and started thinking about her mother. She needed to talk to her; to tell her that she was trying to put her life in order; she would be so happy to hear good news for a change but first she needed to sleep. She slept through that evening and into the next day waking up ready to face the world. She called her mother and arranged to meet her for lunch assuring her that it was good news; not the usual cry of desperation. Noreen's face lit up when she saw Joy walk into the restaurant, gave her a big hug and told her how happy she was to see her. Joy was always amazed at how her mother just kept accepting her no matter what the circumstance. She was ready and willing to do whatever it took to help Joy now that Joy was helping herself.

"You can move back home if you want" she offered with a hint of hesitation in her voice.

Joy declined the offer but did accept some cash to get her through until she got another job. The job proved to be easy enough to get with the help of a friend of her mother's who managed a bank that was hiring new tellers. It wasn't her dream job but the people were nice enough and the work was easy to learn. Bill showed up occasionally and she sent him packing because she knew she couldn't have him in her life anymore. With her first full pay check she moved out of the cockroach-infested apartment into a nicer place in a better part of town and went to the AA meetings just like she was told. Before she had celebrated one month of sobriety after the detox centre, she had launched into a relationship with a guy she met at an AA meeting. He was smooth, young and good-looking and not serious about recovery, either his or Joy's. The relationship became more important than her sobriety and she stopped going to the meetings altogether. Her life began to spiral out of control again, even without the booze, and the bank sent her on stress leave which lasted almost six months.

Over the next year, she made three suicide attempts and was admitted to the hospital psych ward on two other occasions. The doctors did not identify her alcoholism as having any part of her suicidal behavior mainly because she was not drinking throughout this entire year. Instead, they treated her for depression, manic depression, bipolar, anxiety, everything but a serious case of untreated alcoholism.

Things did not seem to be getting any better so Joy decided to try detox again. She remembered how great she felt after that week she spent there so decided to check in for a seven-day outpatient program. She signed in the first morning full of hope; just like the name said "Villa of Hope". This program ran from 8:00 a.m. till 6:00 p.m. every day for seven days and everyone went home each night. At the end of the third day, two of the guys in the program walked with her to the bus stop and lit up a joint on the way.

"You guys are crazy!" Joy said with a big smile on her face. "If they catch you, you're out!"

"So what, who gives a shit" Jason said as he passed it over to her.

She took it between her fingers, put it to her lips and took a big toke, pulling it down into her lungs and holding it there as long as she could. God that felt good! She passed it over to Will and when it came back to her, toked again.

When there was nothing left of the joint, Jason said "Fuck it, let's go for a beer." and they went, all three of them. It just felt like the thing to do.

They had two beers each and then left because nobody had any more money otherwise they probably would have stayed all night. Strangely enough, they all showed up for treatment again the next morning and were promptly dismissed for relapsing. Someone had seen them and ratted them out. Joy could hardly understand what had just happened; it just didn't make sense. She begged the counselor to take her back, fearful for her life and he understood the danger with her hospitalization history, so he admitted her to the twenty-eight day residential program but at the end of the twenty-eight days, she came out just as hopeless and depressed as the day she went in. Joy decided that if this was what being sober was all about, then she would have no part of it and went back to her old ways.

It was New Years Eve and Joy and her friend Trina from the bank had been given tickets to a Gala Party at a swanky nightclub so they got all dolled up and went for it. The party was pretty lame by their standards and they ended up sitting at the bar having the bartender mix them up different fancy drinks one after the other; after all, it wasn't costing them anything. They were starting to get pretty loaded when a good looking guy finally showed up and sat down beside them.

"Having a good time ladies?

Joy and Trina looked at each other and shrugged.

"How about a dance?" the handsome stranger said as he held his hand out for Joy to take.

"Why not" she said as she held on to his hand to help her get to her feet.

They danced all the slow ones for the rest of the night and Trina went home alone in a cab.

Dan and Joy never really fell in love but got married after Joy got pregnant. Being pregnant was enough incentive for Joy to stay sober, but once the baby was born she could not justify abstaining any longer and planned her binges by inviting her mother over on the pretense of visiting. As soon as her mother would show up, she would take off for the bar and not come home till she was completely obliterated. Her mother was not happy with the situation but was grateful to have time with the baby so always showed up when asked. Dan was busy managing a new brew pub and Joy was running the convenience store they had bought a franchise for. They kept pretty busy for a couple of years but they never spent any time together as a family. When they made the mutual decision to split up, Joy got the convenience store in the divorce settlement.

One of her regular suppliers for the store starting coming on to her when he noticed she had no wedding ring anymore and she enjoyed the attention, so agreed to go out for drinks with him. Stan seemed like such a nice guy; so sweet and polite and they dated for about six months before he asked her to marry him.

"Why not?" she thought to herself. "Seems like a good guy. I could do worse" and she said yes. What she did not know about Stan though was that he was not only an alcoholic but a compulsive gambler too. They had both been on their best behavior till now, but the truth would soon come out.

When Stan started asking to borrow money she got suspicious and found out he was feeding the video lottery terminals every chance he got. The money problems grew into an obsession for Joy and she started drinking more and more. Her son practically lived at the day care she took him to which was run by a friend of hers who had unending patience and never complained about him being there too late.

The town they were living in was small and there were only a few places to buy liquor so Joy had to be careful to alternate and rotate and not go to the same place too many times in a row for her supply. Sometimes she would make a big show out of buying a case of wine for a big dinner party or six bottles of tequila for Mexican night, really believing that she was fooling the clerks at the liquor stores. She didn't want anybody to know just how much she was drinking and thought if she bought all kinds of booze they wouldn't think it was all for her because most people just buy certain things over and over but she could drink anything.

One Saturday night, a couple of girlfriends invited her along on a girls night out, so she picked up her son at day care, took him home to stay with a babysitter for the night and went out for a good time. The girls closed the bar down and went to somebody's place a few miles out of town to continue the party and when the party ran out of booze at about 3:00 a.m., Joy stumbled out to her car to leave.

After about three attempts, she finally got the key into the ignition and the car lurched off into the night. Joy was so drunk she could hardly see the road and missed the curve heading under the overpass entirely, smashing head on into the concrete wall under the overpass. Her head went through the windshield and her left hand was completely crushed on impact. Days later, when she woke up in the hospital she was horrified to find out what had happened. She couldn't remember anything; nothing about the party before the accident or the accident itself. Her head hurt so much she wished she was dead; she had lost a quarter of her skull along with the scalp attached to it. There were endless operations to patch up the skull, skin grafts to piece the scalp back together and reconstructive surgeries to rebuild her crushed hand. She felt like Humpty Dumpty.

It took about two years to heal up to the point of feeling almost normal. Joy and Stan sold the store, packed up and moved to another town to try and start fresh; there were too many bad memories to deal with in this town, but Joy soon knew that all her problems had followed her. Stan had taken a new sales rep job that kept him on the road for weeks at a time so Joy was alone a lot now and she was not good on her own, so drank to ease her pain, both physical and emotional. She tried not to drink but she was lonely and just couldn't help it; she needed relief from the unbearable pain. Whenever she drank, it was almost always nearly tragic. She would pass out leaving the oven on and wake up to find the house filling with smoke or wake up to find candles burned down to the nub, wax all over the place; fire always an imminent danger. If she ran out of booze, she would just leave her child home alone and drive to the liquor store or the pub to replenish her supply, knowing full well in the back of her mind that this was wrong but unable to stop herself.

Joy became pregnant for the second time and discovered she was having twins. Once again, she was able to stay sober for the duration of the pregnancy but she always knew that she would drink again as soon as she could. When the twins were six months old she decided it was her time, got a babysitter and went out for drinks with a friend. It felt so incredibly good to be numb again after a few drinks. Her accident had never scared her off driving and she thought nothing of staggering out to her car and hitting the road but her guardian angel must have been watching her that night because a police car pulled her over just a block from the bar and charged her with impaired driving. She didn't argue; got dropped off at home by the police, paid the babysitter and went to bed. It was kind of strange but she didn't feel angry, just tired. She peeled off her clothes and fell into a drugged sleep.

When she woke up the next morning to the sound of babies crying she knew it was over; the drinking had to end. It wasn't just her decision that clinched it though; the court ordered her to enter a three-day detox and attend AA meetings. They gave her a card that she had to have signed by the chairperson of every AA meeting she attended to prove that she had been there. Joy didn't fight it this time. She knew she had hit her bottom and there was nowhere to go but up.

Stan couldn't handle her sober lifestyle, mainly because it made him look bad, and left. Joy and the kids moved again but this time for the right reasons. After her thirteen year battle with the bottle, Joy finally recognized the insane thinking that always preceded that first drink and is happier now than she has ever been in her own skin. She deals with her physical pain in natural ways and her emotional pain has subsided. Her children now have a loving, healthy, sober mother with a future.

The End

# CHAPTER SIX
# SHILO

Shilo's parents emigrated from Germany to a homestead in Saskatchewan in the spring of 1935. Shilo was the middle child; a shy and serious five year old in September of 1939 when Canada declared war on Germany, joining in with the rest of the world. The Germans seemed an alien race to Shilo. She knew nothing about being German or what it meant to the rest of the world at this point in time. All she knew was the fear of the dreaded foreigner enemies coming over the hill and through the trees to slaughter them while they slept in their little log cabin. There was so much to worry about; all anyone ever talked about was rationing, the depression, food shortages, starvation, dust storms, the War and the Germans.

They managed to survive the next few lean years and relocated to a farm closer to a school so that the children could get an education. Shilo had never been anywhere without her parents and was terrified of school. At home, Shilo spent most of her time with her father, following him around the farm, handing him tools, watching him work. It was easy to spend time with him. He was a quiet, patient man who didn't ask a lot of questions. Mother, on the other hand, was loud and bossy and given to anger easily. Shilo did what she could to stay out of her mother's way to avoid the constant reminders of what a sinful child she was; she got enough of that every Sunday at church.

By the time Shilo was fourteen, it was arranged for her to take room and board during the week at a boarding house in town. The rules at the boarding house were very strict: up at six in the morning and out of the house by half past seven, having prepared and eaten breakfast, cleaned up the mess, made all the beds and swept the entire main floor out. Shilo worked for her keep, so after school she came straight back to the boarding house, helped prepare supper for the residents, served the meal, cleaned up the next mess, swept the floors again, then mixed and punched up the bread dough for the next day's breakfast to start all over again.

On weekends, she sometimes went back to the farm with her older sister Nettie and brother-in-law Tom, usually with a jar of the homemade chokecherry wine that Tom's father made. A few months after they had moved to the city for jobs, Nettie had written to her mother begging to come back home to the farm because her life with Tom was so unbearable. Her mother hid the letter away and had no intention of responding to it. When Nettie phoned a few weeks later, Shilo listened as their mother shouted into the phone "You made your bed, now you lie in it!" before she hung the phone up on Nettie. Shilo felt so sorry for Nettie, if her own mother would not help her, then who on earth would? The message was burned into her mind.

When she turned 18, Shilo went to stay with an Aunt in Calgary with hopes of finding a job in the city. In no time at all, she got a job as a telephone operator. There were a lot of young women working for the phone company and she soon made friends. They would go out for lunch to the diner down the street and have the soup of the day with some crackers and coffee for twenty cents, but even more nourishing than the soup was the friendship; the camaraderie with these young women who accepted her as one of them. She was one of the gang and they included her in their plans and even fixed her up with blind dates. Shilo was more than willing to go along on these blind dates because she did not have any idea of how to meet men and was definitely looking for a husband. It wasn't long before she hit the jackpot. One of the blind dates actually asked her to marry him. Of course she said yes without hesitation; a girl would have to be crazy to turn down a proposal. Who knew if you would ever get asked again. She needed to matter to someone; anyone, and this one would do just fine.

Shilo did not have a clue about how she should feel towards the man she had just agreed to spend the rest of her life with; didn't actually know him at all, not really. She had no feelings of affection or love or tenderness, just the desperation of needing a husband. This whole thing didn't feel right or wrong, good or bad; didn't really feel like anything at all. She knew she had already done so many things that were wrong in God's eyes; there surely was a ticket to Hell with her name on it somewhere. She had smoked cigarettes, drank liquor, uttered profanities and even had sex outside the bonds of holy matrimony, so now she needed to make it right with God. Everything would be better soon; she wouldn't be such a sinner in God's eyes if she were married. That was a sacred thing.

They had to move fast. She didn't want anything to go wrong; didn't want to give Wally any time to change his mind, so she took a quick trip back to the farm to pick up her high school graduation dress, the best dress she owned. But she wasn't going to tell anyone in her family about getting married, not going to mention it at all, not to anyone, because it was none of their business and she didn't want them messing it up for her. The wedding was small and uneventful, just a couple of the girls from work and their boyfriends with the Justice of the Peace performing the ceremony and then over to the hotel where everyone, especially Wally, got very drunk.

Six months into the marriage, Wally lost his job because of his drinking and started staying out all night;

not showing up for days on end. Shilo would become frantic when Wally did not come home, phoning the hospitals to see if he had been taken there in a car accident or found dead in the street, calling the police department to see if anything had been reported. If he was gone for three days in a row, she would call the police and file a missing persons report. The most frightening part of the possibility of something happening to Wally was the thought of being left alone. Life with Wally was far from good but it was still better than being alone and an uncomfortable, desperate feeling began to overwhelm her almost all the time. There was no way she could tell what her emotions were; happy, sad, fear, anger, shame; they all felt the same, they all felt bad.

Wally was now disappearing for weeks on end so Shilo decided they had to move; had to get Wally away from the bad influence of his drinking buddies and she convinced him that they should just pack up and move to Toronto.

Shilo got a job with another phone company shortly after they moved, where she sat next to a girl called Marie who invited her out for drinks after work with her and the rest of the girls for their regular Friday night get together. From that first night out, she never missed a Friday night out with the girls; it was not as if anyone would be home waiting anyway. It hadn't taken Wally five minutes to find new low-life friends of his own at the job he got as a janitor at the bus depot.

"Why shouldn't I have a little fun now and then", she would say to her new friends after a couple of drinks. After a few more, it would start to feel so good; such a release from the misery, her self-confidence boosted, no fear, no guilt, no shame, so in control, just out having fun with the girls. On the nights she was not out having fun with the girls, she was still the dutiful little wife making supper for her husband, but when he didn't show up by six o'clock, which was more often than not, she would feed his supper to the neighbor's dog. She spent a lot of supper hours with that dog and started to believe that she liked the dog more than she liked Wally. Wally just couldn't seem to hold on to any work, no matter how easy it was, and lost job after job. There was always some really good reason for him to lose those jobs; the demanding asshole supervisor who fired him for missing too much work; the bitch in payroll who reported him for swearing at her; whatever it was, it was always someone else's fault, never his.

Time for another geographical cure. They should go to Ottawa where Wally had a brother. Maybe that would be better; maybe a little family around would be a good influence on him. Wally's brother came out and helped them pack up their belongings, furniture and all, and away the two brothers drove while Shilo stayed behind in the empty apartment sleeping in an old sleeping bag on the floor while she worked off her last few days at the phone company. Wally would find them an apartment in Ottawa and get it all set up for her arrival.

There was a tearful farewell party for Shilo at the hotel bar with the girls from work. It was for the best they all agreed; probably straighten Wally right out they said. His brother will keep an eye on him for you now, they were all sure. When she arrived at the bus station in Ottawa, no one was there to meet her, so she phoned Wally's brother to pick her up and take her over to the new apartment. Their new home turned out to be a real dump of a place with only half of their furniture in it. When Wally showed up an hour later he confessed to having sold some of their stuff because he hadn't been able to get a job as quick as he thought and was running low on money. Something snapped inside Shilo and she was in a rage.

She threw her suitcase in Wally's general direction as hard as she could and it smashed against the wall, flinging open and spilling her clothes onto the floor. "You selfish bastard! Don't you care about anything except yourself? How are we supposed to live in this hole with nothing? Why did I even come here?" she wailed as she slumped down on one of the two tattered kitchen chairs left. Wally didn't answer; he was long gone out the door. He wasn't going to listen to this bullshit, not for a minute.

Well he couldn't hold a job but she could. She got on with Wilson's Department Store in the customer service department as a file clerk. There were about a dozen young women in the general office and a bunch of them would walk the three blocks at lunch time on Fridays over to a bar for sandwiches and a couple of drinks. These lunches were usually stretched out longer than the normal lunch period into at least an hour and a half. In that time, Shilo could usually down three drinks while smoking one cigarette after the other. The food was not important; it didn't make her feel any better, but the beer; she loved the beer. It made her feel as though she fit in with these big city girls who were so sophisticated. They knew just how to hold a cigarette to look oh so glamorous and they knew the names of all the drinks that sounded so exotic. She caught on quick when she drank and got funnier and prettier and much smarter too. All the disappointment of life with Wally disappeared for a while. The only bad part of Friday lunches were the Friday afternoons back at the office. Nothing much would be accomplished on those afternoons. It was all she could do to stay awake and look alive till five o'clock when they could head back to the bar because after all, it was Friday.

Life went on in the shabby little apartment. They bought some more cheap furniture with her paychecks and Shilo tried to make the place as livable as possible, sewing curtains and polishing up the old, cracked linoleum. Wally worked here and there and drank up most of his money. Life was a chore except for Fridays and then winter came. A poster went up at the office that said they were looking for ladies for the Saturday morning curling league; just a fun league; no pressure to be good or anything, so she signed her name on the sheet.

Two weeks later she showed up at the Granite Curling Club bright and early Saturday morning. As usual, Wally was nowhere to be found so she didn't even have to fight with him to get out the door. She knew a bit about curling but never knew how much fun it could be. There were lots of laughs and the women all shared jokes and jibes about their husbands or their boyfriends. Shilo never said much about Wally; she was too embarrassed and no matter what kind of losers the other girls said they had, their husbands showed up when they were supposed to and held down jobs and probably even came home every night. But the best part came after the curling game was over, when they all headed for the lounge upstairs in the curling rink.

By the time three o'clock rolled around, all the other curlers had gone home, but Shilo was still there, very drunk. The bartender stuffed her into a cab and managed to get her address out of her so she made it home in one piece and passed out across the bed for the rest of that day and night.

The next morning she woke up not only with a pounding hangover, but with the deepest feeling of shame and guilt she had ever known. The shame was overwhelming. She had never felt so alone. This was all Wally's fault; if he was a proper husband she wouldn't be doing these things. But what could she do, she knew the rules, the very words of her mother "You made your bed, now you lie in it". There was no one to confide in because to do that she would have to confess everything and that was far too shameful. Somehow she managed to live through that day and the next day and a few more until she started to feel human again.

Shilo's sister-in-law Ruthie felt sorry for the poor girl being alone so much and eventually invited her to come along to the Legion Hall to play bingo. Shilo discovered that the bingo games (where the prizes were never more than two dollars) were not the main attraction here. Cheap drinks. That was the draw for this crowd. Everyone seemed to be having such a good time; a few games of bingo and a couple of beer and soon Shilo was at the legion three nights a week and it wasn't for the potential fortune in bingo jackpots. There were lots of lonely people looking for solace at that legion hall and she enjoyed the company.

The fact that she was drinking regularly now was not a concern to her, but what she did know was that Wally was responsible for all of her problems. He never hurt her physically but he would abuse her verbally without mercy.

He would come home drunk and boast about the other women he had been with. Practically all they did now was fight and accuse each other of all the unseemly things they could think of. Anything Shilo accused Wally of was probably justified but the things that Wally was accusing her of were ridiculous.

"You whore! Who did you screw last night? I saw you coming out of the legion with some guy! Did he pay you? Give me your purse!" Wally would then grab her purse and rip it open to get any money he could get his hands on.

She soon learned not to keep what little money she had in her purse. After a while, a kind of numbness took over her insides and she just went through the days like a robot, but a couple of drinks always seemed to kick start her heart, so she started hanging around the legion more and more. Sometimes, when the lights were flashing for last call, some fellow traveler would offer her a ride home; she would accept and end up at some cheap motel with him. It was so easy to justify; she had already been accused of the crime so she might as well commit it. It was just a little tenderness in her lonely world, but the cold light of dawn brought it all back. That ticket to Hell with her name on it was still there, still doomed for eternity.

The guilt and shame were almost doing her in when somehow, through all the turmoil, she became pregnant with Wally's baby. She knew it was his because she counted back the days. He was working as a waiter on the passenger trains then and was away for two weeks at a time, then back for three days. When she counted back, it had been a weekend when he was home and they had gotten drunk together so they must have conceived a child in that drunken stupor.

"This will be good for us" she told her friends at work. "It'll make Wally more responsible; being a father and all".

When baby James was born, Wally was away on the trains and within another month he had lost that job too. No sooner was he unemployed again than the disappearing act resumed. When he was home, they still got drunk together because that's all they had in common, and within the next year she had another child, a girl. Shilo went back to work within six weeks after the birth of both babies because she had to. The thing about working and having babies was that it did keep her away from the curling rink and the legion but, still somehow, things went from bad to worse. Shilo moved out on Wally before the baby girl turned one.

Some friends from the legion called her up for old times sake one afternoon and convinced her to come down for a few and forget about her troubles for a while. Wally's Dad had given her a hundred dollars for the babies but she figured she could use just a little of the money for herself, she was feeling so awful. That was probably the shortest night out she ever had. Within hours she was rushed to the hospital to find out that she had infectious hepatitis. What followed was a couple of years of collecting welfare and babysitting other people's kids to try and make ends meet. Shilo and her two small children moved often trying to get away from Wally, but he found them every time and promised to straighten out if she would just take him back. Shilo finally caved in and let him come back. She had been staying away from the booze because of her poor health and without it to drown the loneliness and fear she was so vulnerable. There was no way on earth she could have said no; she was so low at this point. She was scared to drink because of how sick she had gotten the last time but she really had no idea of how to handle life's problems without a crutch.

With Wally back, nothing changed like she had hoped; things were just the same as before so she went to a doctor hoping he could fix all her problems. The doctor she saw decided she needed a tranquilizer and prescribed Valium. Without a second thought, down they went, pill after pill, day after day until there wasn't a day she could survive without them. After about a year on Valium she started to feel like a zombie but didn't really worry too much about it. The Valium helped her deal with all of Wally's moving in and out, or her kicking him out then begging him to come back over and over like a stuck record. As far as she could tell, the Valium worked.

Now that she had a crutch to help her out, Shilo found a job, but there were no friendly faces there; no Friday nights to look forward to. It started out with an innocent stop at the liquor store on the way home from work one hot Friday afternoon and soon it was Friday and Monday and Wednesday whether Wally was around or not. The beer was back.

In the summer, she could wander around the yard of the house she rented, dig a little in the garden, pull out a few weeds, cut some grass and then reward herself with a cold beer in the shade and that's how it went. The yard looked good and she got what she wanted, numb. Then the snow flew so she sat in an armchair in front of the picture window and found the numbness there.

The kids were now teenagers getting into all kinds of trouble and the school was calling regularly but what could she do? "Yes, yes I'll deal with it" she would tell the school counselor even though she knew she just couldn't do it. It always erupted into more fighting between her and the kids and nothing good ever came out of the confrontations so she avoided them.

Shilo was at work the day the tow truck hauled the car away, repossessed. The car was still in Wally's name and he hadn't kept up the payments so off it went, further proof of what a loser Wally was. The stress of dealing with Wally's craziness and the kids' getting into trouble was starting to get to her; the Valium just wasn't cutting it anymore. Time to try a new doctor. She found a doctor who seemed sympathetic to her plight. "I just can't sleep at night" she told the doctor. "My husband is a drunk who is verbally abusive and gets into all kinds of trouble and causes me nothing but pain. My kids won't listen to me and I need to quit smoking."

Shilo thought if she could just quit smoking she wouldn't be in so much physical pain and would be able to deal with situations better. The doctor found nothing physically wrong with her but did prescribe a mild sleeping pill. The beauty of this pill was that whenever she ran out, she could just call the pharmacy up and they would refill it, so every night she would slosh down a few with a couple of beers. For health reasons, she even sacrificed beer and switched completely to red wine for a while.

Eventually, she talked to a lawyer, filed for a legal separation from Wally and started divorce proceedings. He contested the divorce, demanding that she pay him support. She had full custody of the two kids and stayed in the home they had been living in. He got nothing and left.

The unknown is probably the most frightening thing there is, and that's how it was for Shilo. Even as bad as life with Wally was, she had come to know what to expect; it was at least predictable. But now what? She soon filled that gap with another drunk she met at the legion. He said a few kind words to her and she was his! This guy was a real prize. Steve lived in a tiny apartment on the third floor of an old rooming house with his two adult sons, a teenage daughter and a huge German Shepherd with an untrained puppy. The dogs were never let outside, so the apartment was disgusting to say the least. Steve's claim to fame was that he was expecting a large insurance settlement, which should be coming through any day now. This made the package all the more attractive to Shilo so she wasted no time moving him and one of his sons in to her house.

Her kids could not stand Steve and his son but she didn't care, she had her man and the man had a settlement coming. They drank and fought and drank some more until she was the one who became physically abusive toward him. One night after a particularly irritating fight with Steve, she told him to get out so he went down to the basement and starting throwing his clothes into a garbage bag. She panicked at the prospect of being alone again, couldn't bear the thought, grabbed the garbage bag out of his hand, emptied all his clothes into the washing machine and turned it on.

"That should keep him from leaving" she thought to herself. Within minutes, they started fighting again and she was yelling "GET OUT GET OUT JUST GET OUT" as she was pulling the sloshing clothes out of the washing machine, water slopping all over the floor. After she managed to ram all the dripping wet clothes back into the garbage bag, she heaved it at him.

He took the bag full of sopping clothes and left. She couldn't believe her eyes. He left!

A few days later, she was at the legion crying to Steve, "Please come back, I need you". But Steve was fixed up for the night and told her to get lost. Usually, it didn't take long for Steve's latest girlfriend to sober up and realize the prize she had and that the famous "settlement" was never going to materialize. Then it was his turn to beg Shilo to take him back. One night before Steve drove off in a fit of fury, she put sugar in his gas tank while he was packing up his garbage bags, not really sure whether it was to keep him from leaving or to keep him from coming back. He never came back.

Wally was now harassing Shilo and the kids to the point where she had to get a restraining order against him. All this aggravation increased her need to kill the pain of all this misery. It seemed there was nothing that would fill the huge emptiness inside her. The drinking, the smoking, the tranquilizers and the sleeping pills continued till it got to the point where she felt so emotionally bankrupt and so utterly lonely that she didn't want to live anymore so she went to see another doctor.

She told the doctor of her troubles with these men in her life and her unruly children and how badly she still needed to quit smoking. "Maybe if I can quit smoking, I'll feel better" she offered.

"How much do you smoke?" the Doctor asked.

"Oh, I'm up to two packs a day now" she wheezed.

"How much alcohol do you drink?" the Doctor asked, busy writing something down in her notepad.

"Well……" Shilo proceeded to tell the Doctor about her drinking habits. She really didn't think that drinking had anything to do with the way she felt so she had no reason to lie about the drinking.

The Doctor sat quietly for a moment reading the notes she had just written and said "Shilo, I think that you would definitely benefit from attending Alcoholics Anonymous meetings."

Shilo's first thought was "Well, that's ridiculous! I don't have a problem with alcohol!" but she didn't actually say it out loud. She respected the Doctor so all she said was "OK. What do I do?"

The doctor suggested she call the Alcoholism Foundation and they would tell her where to find an AA meeting close to where she lived. She called the number that same day.

At 7:30 that night, Shilo made her way over to a church where a meeting was scheduled. There was a sign on the door that said "AA Meeting Downstairs" so down the stairs she went. It was odd, she thought, she wasn't even nervous or apprehensive about this. It was like she was being guided through the whole experience. She heard voices down the hall and headed for the sound. There were probably fifteen or twenty people in various stages of sitting, standing and milling around a circle of metal folding chairs; most with a paper cup of coffee in one hand and a cigarette in the other. So far so good, she walked into the room, poured herself a coffee and lit a cigarette. Within a few minutes they all started sitting down so she sat down too. The meeting was set into motion and she heard people talk about doing time in jail, getting sent to the psych ward, landing in the hospital, losing drivers' licenses, losing families, losing jobs, bad car accidents, death and destruction, on and on; all because of their drinking. She could not identify with any of these people! She had not done any of these things. Their lives were way more messed up than hers; smoking was her biggest problem. But then someone started talking about feelings. Fear, anger, resentment, shame, guilt, loneliness. The words stabbed at her and she thought 'Oh my God, maybe these people can help me!" Something was beginning to click into place as she lit another cigarette and remembered the doctor saying that she shouldn't worry about quitting smoking just now.

She stayed sober for a few months, attending lots of meetings but it wasn't that easy. In mid-summer she was offered a transfer to another city with a decent increase in salary and could not refuse. Even if she stayed sober here, she felt as though she was still in a rut.

Over the years Shilo had become practically estranged from most of her family so it was a real shock when she got a call from her mother to say that they were coming for a visit. Her mother, father, sister and two nieces showed up the next night. The stress was too much; she couldn't handle it and picked up a six-pack of beer before they arrived and quickly drank four by herself. The next night she picked up a dozen beer on her way home from work and it was the same for the next four days of their visit. When they left five days later, she knew she had to get back to the AA meetings, but felt so ashamed and didn't know if she could swallow enough pride to get there. It took a couple of weeks but she made it back to the same meeting that she had gone to the very first time. It felt okay. No one shunned her or made her feel any worse than she already did. They actually welcomed her and told her it was good that she was back.

At the last meeting she attended before she moved, the group presented her with a farewell card they had all signed and put their phone numbers on. They told her that if she needed to talk to someone, to feel free to use the numbers. She was overcome with emotion and just stood there trying not to cry. She found the meetings near her new home and started going immediately but always made sure she would arrive just before the meeting started and bolt for the door as soon as the meeting was over, then go home thinking "They aren't a very friendly bunch. They sure don't seem to put themselves out to make me feel welcome." One night, someone touched her arm just as she was bolting for the door and invited her to go for coffee with the rest of them. That was all she needed to feel like she was really part of something and that felt pretty good.

A few years into sobriety, Shilo actually managed to quit smoking after countless unsuccessful attempts and many, many partial packs of cigarettes flung out the car window in the midst of a coughing fit. Life was good now as long as she stayed out of sick relationships but she didn't want to go through the rest of her life avoiding relationships so she joined another group called Fresh Start that focused on grieving relationships. Here she uncovered a lot of the baggage she had been toting around. Life was getting better and better all the time; sometimes she couldn't believe how comfortable she felt; this had never been a normal condition for Shilo. There was this thing called serenity; just saying the word was soothing. The idea that not having alcohol in her life meant no more fun; no more excitement, had turned out to be all wrong. Without the booze, she found a new freedom to do the things she had always been so afraid to try. She learned to live naturally, without chemicals to control her waking and sleeping. The constant chaos of her life was replaced with sanity.

Shilo learned to be still and listen; especially at her favorite spot on a cliff overlooking the river where she would often see a pair of eagles. One calm, sunny morning as she sat on a rock hoping to catch a glimpse of the eaglet she thought they might have hatched, the male eagle circled above her, made two great flaps and dropped a twenty-inch wing feather near her feet. She has never questioned her path in life again.

The End

# CHAPTER SEVEN
# LYLYJA

Lylyja was born in a little village in Minnesota on New Year's Day of 1930 to hard working immigrant parents from Iceland, the only sister for five brothers. The family was known as a pillar of the community; well respected, active members of the local Lutheran church. Being the baby of the family and the only girl, Lylyja was completely spoiled; always able to get whatever she wanted, especially from the father who doted on her. There was never any alcohol allowed in the family home even though Icelanders are known for their love of spirits; probably something to do with the long, dark months of winter, but they also loved their strong, hot coffee and company was always happy to accept a cup of the thick, black brew permanently percolating on the wood stove. Lylyja's brothers were not tea totallers like their parents though; they wanted more excitement than a coffee party and went along with the crowd that liked to have a good time, usually with someone's home brew or homemade wine but they never, ever drank at home out of respect for their parents.

Lylyja had her first taste of alcohol at age ten. A couple of older boys at school dared her to take a drink from the bottle they were passing back and forth in the bushes behind the school at recess one day. She had no idea what it was that they were drinking, but could not refuse a dare and took the bottle.

"Come on Lylyja, we dare you, take a drink!" the boys taunted, shoving the bottle at her. She took a swallow. It was really sweet, cool and warm at the same time. She passed the bottle back to the boys.

"Don't be such a baby Lylyja! Drink some more, come on!"

Lylyja took back the bottle and drank as much as she could before she ran out of breath and held it out in front of her triumphantly. Suddenly she felt disoriented, dizzy and unsteady on her feet. She put her head down, closing her eyes for a moment and when she looked up, the boys had disappeared, leaving her there alone. The bell was ringing; recess was over. She crashed unsteadily back through the bushes to the door of the little school and weaved her way to the back of the room where her empty desk sat. The boys were sitting in the next row across from her desk with their hands covering their mouths giddy with the expectation of getting someone in trouble and getting away with it. All eyes were on the girl slamming into her seat, fumbling around with her books. The teacher turned around from writing on the blackboard when she heard the tittering, quickly saw the reason for the commotion and moved to Lylyja's side, took a look at her flushed face and told her "You go straight home and tell your mother that you are coming down with the mumps. Go now!" Lylyja obeyed and made her way home.

When she arrived home, Lylyja's mother told her to go straight upstairs to bed and she would call Amma, her grandmother. Amma was a sort of midwife nurse and lived just next door so Lylyja's mother went immediately to fetch her.

Amma took one look at Lylyja, sniffed at her face and pronounced loudly in Icelandic "This child has been drinking something! There are no mumps! She has been drinking dandelion wine. She is not sick but she is drunk!"

Amma was furious. Lylyja's mother was mortified; a child of hers sent home from school for drinking alcohol; it was scandalous and could not be tolerated. Profuse apologies would have to be made to the teacher and the principal before Lylyja would be allowed to return to school the next morning to the smirks and snarls of the rest of the students.

By the time Lylyja was fourteen, she was teaching Sunday school at the church on Sunday mornings after regularly drinking dandelion wine the Saturday nights before. Unfortunately for her, this pattern did not go unnoticed and one particularly hung over Sunday morning, the Pastor of the church asked Lylyja to stay after the Sunday school class was over.

"I need your resignation as teacher of the Sunday school class." he announced firmly as she walked into his office at the back of the church. Lylyja was dumbfounded.

"But why, what have I done wrong?" she asked him as calmly as she could.

He stood up, turned his back to her and refused to say anymore.

Lylyja stood her ground "I absolutely refuse to give you my resignation. I have done nothing wrong!"

The Pastor whirled around and spat out "Then I will resign for you and no one will ever know the difference!"

With teeth clenched, Lylyja slowly told him "Fine then, the next time I come into this church, it will be in a box!" and she walked out of that church for the last time.

Her parents noticed that something was wrong when she got home but Lylyja refused to talk about it, asking that they just leave her alone. The next Sunday, the Pastor announced that the Sunday school teacher had resigned and then her parents knew. They sat there in shame knowing that it was their daughter he was talking about and that she must have done something horribly wrong to be in this situation. This was a small village;

everyone would know soon enough and they would not forget easily. Lylyja seriously questioned her faith now; this was a hard knock to take, the church had been a big part of her life but was not her friend any longer.

When Lylyja turned sixteen, her parents began to be concerned with her wild nature and felt that she needed to be controlled more. She had a lot of freedom in the small village and all her friends were there, some of whom were definitely bad influences with their rough ways. The decision was made that a boarding school would be preferable to all this freedom and they sent her away to St. Mary's Academy in Minneapolis where she lived for two years, coming home only for holidays and the occasional extended weekend. Lylyja learned a lot at the boarding school and not just how to behave like a proper young lady.

After graduation, Lylyja got a job in the city as a sales clerk where she could earn enough money of her own to get into real trouble. Her freedom didn't last long though, once her father found out just exactly what she was up to. He drove into the city and brought her straight home; shamed once again. Her father put her to work at the post office he managed and paid her enough to keep her and her friends in beer most of the time but when it wasn't enough, she stole what she needed from him.

Lylyja met Andy just before her twentieth birthday. Andy was a heavy drinker so Lylyja did not have to worry about being criticized for her own drinking and they fell in love. They caused a huge scandal in the village by living together in a little rented house on the edge of town without the benefit of holy matrimony. Over the next ten years, they cohabited off and on, moving into a bigger house now and then as Lylyja produced seven sons, most of whom did not resemble Andy. Their home was always nothing short of chaotic at any point in time with all the drinking and fighting and kids all over the place.

Lylyja's father still loved and watched over his only daughter and now worried not only about her, but about his grandsons as well. He would regularly go to their house and take some of the kids home with him for a while, away from the drinking and the fighting, fearing for their wellbeing. Lylyja and Andy's drinking was getting them in trouble with the law more and more often now and every time she was in trouble, Lylyja's father would pay the fines and bail her out. He usually let Andy sit in jail but he always bailed Lylyja out after they had been charged with some minor offence. The crimes were usually driving impaired, fighting in public or disturbing the peace. Often, the police threw them in cells just to sober up and things just kept getting worse and worse as the years went by and the number of kids went up.

When Lylyja's father passed away in 1960, her whole world fell apart. She had depended on him for her life; he was her safety net. The only person who was always there for her, no matter what, was gone forever. Now there was no one who cared enough to look out for her and her children. Lylyja was inconsolable and stayed drunk for weeks, unable to cope with the loss of her beloved father.

In that hazy period after her father's death, Lylyja was out looking for the bootlegger one night, pounding and cursing at the closed door of a house in the village that no one would answer, totally unaware that the door was, in fact, the police constable's door. Finally, a woman answered the door and politely invited Lylyja in. The woman was the constable's wife and she kept Lylyja there until the officer returned, lying to her that the bootlegger would be right back with a supply. When the constable returned, Lylyja offered no resistance; she was so drunk and worn out that she could hardly stand as they locked her up in the cell.

Andy had been caught earlier that night after a car chase through the country side driving a stolen car until it ran out of gas and had been locked up in a neighboring town, awaiting his appointment with a judge for sentencing.

Because this was such a small town, everyone knew everyone else and the constable's wife knew that Lylyja and Andy had a bunch of kids who might be left home alone so she called Lylyja's mother and advised her to collect them and take them home with her; Lylyja wasn't going anywhere and her father could not bail her out this time.

The oldest five children were sent to live with various relatives for the time being, but the two youngest were taken into custody by Family Services. One child was three years old and the other just six months old. They were now Wards of the Court and Lylyja would have to fight hard to get her two youngest sons back.

Her day in court came the next day and the presiding Judge took note of how sick and sad Lylyja looked and asked the arresting officer to get her a glass of water and an aspirin. The two babies were in the courtroom with their Amma and they were crying out to her, wanting their mother, but she was not allowed to go near them. Lylyja had not felt heartache like that since her father's death. The Judge decided to let her go home with a warning to abstain from alcohol and appear in court the following week for sentencing but meanwhile, the two youngest children were taken back into custody.

Lylyja was crushed; she could not believe that they were taking away her babies. As bad as her drinking was, she always loved her babies and tried her best to look after them. A week later, at the sentencing, she got thirty days in jail because she couldn't pay the fines and the Judge ordered an officer to take her away.

As the officer led her to the paddy wagon heading for the jail, he stood back, looked at her and said "You have two beautiful little boys there."

Lylyja looked at him with the saddest eyes he had ever seen and said "And what's going to happen to them now?"

He told her "You have a drinking problem. Do something about it before you lose them and your other kids too."

The color drained from her face as she looked straight into his eyes and said "If that's the case, I've taken my last drink."

The two smallest children were kept in care for six months. The prosecutor wanted a year but it almost seemed as though he sensed the difference in Lylyja since he last saw her and did not oppose the decision.

From the day she told that police officer she had taken her last drink, she kept her word. She never touched another drop, got all her kids back in six months and never had to go through anything like that ever again.

Lylyja's journey into sobriety began that day in 1960. Once she was back home with her children, the first thing she did was to search out one of her brothers; one who had given up drinking. She needed some guidance. Her brother and a friend of his talked late into the night and her head was swimming by the time they left. The next morning, as she tried to recollect some of the conversation, she found she could not remember much of what was said except "always keep an open mind". That seemed like good advice and she took heed. They took her to an AA meeting a few days later at someone's home.

Lylyja was very scared at this point but there was another person there for the first time and she thought "If he can do it, so can I". Every week after that, someone would pick her up because she had no license to drive, and take her to an AA meeting. She was the only female at all of the meetings in the whole countryside until 1978.

For eighteen years she was the only woman who had the courage to attend the meetings, but the men at those meetings taught her a lot about how to live a good life. As time went on and the membership grew (still no women), the meetings moved out of people's homes into church basements and halls. They would pile into someone's car and drive all over the country to all the meetings there were, never identifying themselves by name, even though everyone probably knew all their names anyway. After about seven years and hundreds of meetings, Lylyja figured she could stay sober on her own without the AA fellowship and did manage for a while until her insides were turning upside down and she knew she had to go back.

Andy remained a part of her life always. He was in and out of recovery until he was diagnosed with terminal cancer and she took him home to nurse him through to the end. The Pastor came to see her during this time and prayed with her to save Andy's soul. The old hurt associated with the church welled up and turned to anger as she told the Pastor "That won't do much good as there is no God or that man wouldn't be suffering the way he is!" Later, in reminiscence, she decided that God must actually have been listening because Andy got his rest a few days later.

The pastor came to see her again after Andy died and she softened up a bit as he said "I believe I have seen you at open AA meetings; are you a member?"

Lylyja said "Yes, I am" and that felt good.

After Andy's death, Lylyja turned back to the fellowship of AA for solace and started doing more service work. Looking back over the years, Lylyja felt that she had a very happy, joyous and free life in spite of everything and truly enjoyed the journey living the way AA taught and was eternally grateful for that.

Lylyja passed away suddenly of heart failure at 77 years of age, a sober member of AA for an incredible 47 years, a genuine pioneer for women of sobriety.

*Rest in Peace Lylyja*
*We will always remember you*

The End

# CHAPTER EIGHT
# MIRIAM

Miriam had known for over a year where her birth mother was but had done nothing with the information, just filed it away in the back of her mind until she felt ready to deal with it. That knowledge was heavy on her mind as she started thinking about how the world could end without her ever having dealt with such a huge issue and decided that it was time to see her mother face to face before it was too late. Her aunts told her that they knew where her mother was; that she was living in Toronto. The decision came easily. Miriam bought a Greyhound bus ticket. The trip was unbelievably long and just as she thought she couldn't bear another minute on the bus, the driver announced that they would be pulling in to Toronto in twenty minutes. A feeling of panic crept over her. What was she doing here? What kind of insane idea was this anyway? She did not really remember anything about her mother and had no idea how she would find her or anyone else for that matter in this monstrous city. Miriam was suddenly terrified of what she might find as she stepped off the bus into the heart of the biggest city she had ever seen. Overwhelmed with the enormity of the place, she tried to keep calm and headed for the bank of phone booths across the terminal, hoisting the heavy backpack over her shoulder. Standing in line behind the first pay phone, she glanced nervously around her, not sure of what she was expecting to see. A middle aged woman standing in the line next to her smiled warmly when she saw Miriam scanning the crowd. Miriam tried to smile back but just couldn't.

The woman took a step over and quietly asked "Are you okay? You look a little troubled." Miriam felt instinctively that this woman meant her no harm and she answered "I just got here and I don't know where to start. I'm trying to find my mother and some of my aunties have heard that she is here in Toronto."

Miriam's eyes moistened as the woman reached over and put her hand lightly on her shoulder.

"Well, I may be able to help you there" the kind face replied. "I work with the Christian Women's League and we often help locate missing people." "Maybe you can give me a little more information. Let's just sit over here on a bench and see what we can do."

The woman led Miriam over to a bench where she helped her remove the heavy backpack and set it down. Miriam was grateful to have a friendly face to talk to but leery all the same, having heard about all the weirdoes and bad people in the big city. They sat down side by side on the bench as Miriam explained how she had not seen her mother in twenty-one years; not since Annie had abandoned her family when Miriam was just six years old, leaving her sisters and brothers with their father on their reserve. Miriam's family was Dene. The woman smiled and told Miriam that she was not familiar with the Dene people, so Miriam told her that Dene means "The People". Europeans called them Chipewyan meaning "caribou meat eaters", but they were really Dene; nomads following the seasons and the caribou, living off the land.

Miriam's father Patrick and his side of the family still lived the traditional life on the trap lines, hunting and fishing. None of them spoke English but her mother's family spoke English they had learned at residential schools. Her mother and all the other members of the family had been forcibly taken to residential schools and taught to speak English. Most of them only went to grade four, but Miriam's mother Annie managed to finish grade nine. Grandmother had done her best to hold on to the traditional way of life and continued to tan hides, dry meat and do her beautiful beadwork. It was all she had left.

When Miriam was finished talking, the woman thanked her for sharing her story and suggested that Miriam start looking for her mother by calling the shelters. Her aunts had given her the names of a couple of places they knew Annie had stayed at in the past and the Christian woman said that sometimes people return to the same places again and again so Miriam started with those. The second number she called sounded hopeful. There was an aboriginal woman named Annie who was staying there at the moment, so the person on the phone told Miriam to come over and see if she recognized her.

The woman named Annie was called in to the visitor area unaware of who was looking for her, having been told only that there was someone to see her. She walked in and seemed to recognize Miriam after a moment. They stared at each other in silence then hugged awkwardly, but there was nothing there; no warmth or emotion. They sat down on opposite ends of the hard brown vinyl couch in the visitors' lounge and stared at each other for a few moments. Miriam tried to get Annie to talk about why she had left them all those years ago but Annie refused to talk about any of it. Her brick wall was unmovable. She told Miriam that she wrote out her life story years before, but she destroyed it. Oh, how Miriam wished she could have read it. Miriam didn't stay long. Annie made it clear she wasn't exactly moved by her daughter's appearance after all these years.

Because she was so highly educated with her nine grades of residential school, Miriam's mother Annie had become the first Dene person to work at the reserve school as a teacher's assistant. Miriam's father Patrick was not educated in the ways of the English and the marriage of a purely traditional Dene man and an Anglified Dene woman was highly unusual in the 1950's, especially on a remote northern reserve. Joining the two cultures would prove immensely difficult.

By the time the fifth child, Miriam, was born, Red Dog Lake Reserve had a clinic, a school, a church and a Hudson's Bay store that sold dry goods, groceries and still had a viable fur trade. The reserve was very isolated from the rest of the world; there were no roads to enter or leave from. The only way out was by airplane or dog sled and the nearest airport was 200 miles away. The Hudson's Bay Company store had goods delivered once every two weeks by plane and if anyone needed to leave, that was their best option apart from dog sled in the winter. Winter encompassed a good nine months of the year so dog sledding was still an important mode of transportation.

One of Miriam's first memories as a child was of a winter journey by dog sled, sleeping the nights in a canvas tent with evergreen boughs covering the floor of snow. On this particular journey, Miriam's mother held her on her lap in the back of the sled buried in blankets with her father at the front guiding the dogs. As they were crossing the frozen lake, Patrick brought the sled to an abrupt halt and yanked Annie and Miriam out of the sled and half carried, half pulled them over to the edge of the shore. They stood there stunned and watched as he ran back onto the frozen lake. Everything was ghostly silent for a second and then they heard it, the eerie groaning and snapping of the thick ice layer. Annie held Miriam tight as they stood there terrified, transfixed at what they were seeing. The sled was starting to sink, being pulled backwards into a widening crack as the two dogs closest to the sled were scrambling with all their might against being pulled backwards inch by inch into the icy water. The other six dogs were standing firm. Patrick ordered them to STAY and they did. The two dogs in trouble were now yelping and crying, scratching furiously at the edge of the ice trying to get out of the freezing water. Patrick knew exactly what to do. He slid over toward the opening in the ice on his belly and with adrenaline fueled strength, pushed the sled as far away from the hole as he could, all the while yelling at the dogs in Dene to GO FORWARD, STOP, GO FORWARD, STOP. The dogs obeyed. They trusted him with their lives. Patrick then slid his body around and pulled on the dogs' leads at the same time ordering them to pull with him. It worked! Both dogs were out of the water. They were encased in icy fur coats but they would survive thanks to Patrick's skill as a sledder. He had saved all their lives.

Friends and neighbors envied Miriam's family but things are not always as they seem and that was the case behind the closed doors of Miriam's home. Annie loved her job as the teacher's assistant at the school and was rarely home; her job was her life now. Her children and husband came a distant second and she neglected them greatly. Patrick had always been a drinker, but his drinking increased with his wife's absence and if he was not drunk at home he was out somewhere else getting drunk. The children were never alone though; there was always someone from their extended families staying with them and one night it was Miriam's cousin Jimmy.

Jimmy had gone snooping through the cupboards and found a bottle of wine that he decided to polish off. As soon as Miriam saw him drinking the wine, she hustled the other kids off to bed all in the same room and made sure they were sleeping before she climbed into her parents' bed by herself. She had closed the bedroom door as quietly as she could so she wouldn't attract his attention and tiptoed over to the bed and pulled back the covers. She was in bed for a few minutes before allowing herself to believe she could fall asleep when the bedroom door swung open and banged against the wall. Miriam turned to face the noise. The wine had aroused his adolescent libido and he stood there in the doorway leering at the tiny girl in the bed, his mind imagining what was beneath Miriam's thin nightgown.

Jimmy stepped forward and slammed the door behind him, moving closer to Miriam as she tried to back up, holding the blanket around her, the wall stopping her retreat. With one hand he grabbed her left arm and pushed her back down onto the bed. She pushed back with all her might but could not budge him as he held her right arm with his other hand and fell down on top of her. He outweighed her by at least a hundred pounds. He told her that if she didn't keep quiet that he would kill her and she understood that. She decided she didn't want to be killed and kept quiet while he pulled her nightgown up and pulled his pants down with one hand while the other hand kept her pinned down on the bed.

Miriam started to cry and he told her again "Shut up or I WILL kill you!" She closed her eyes and pretended to be somewhere else. Jimmy found his target and thrust and pounded the little body. Miriam was exploding with pain and tried to imagine in her mind that she was outside skipping rope with her friends when she heard a roar that sounded like a bear as the weight was pulled off her. She opened her eyes to see her father throwing her cousin across the room like a sack of rotten potatoes. She struggled to her feet even though her whole body was trembling uncontrollably. By the time she looked up, the room was empty and the door was closed, as though nothing had happened, as if time had stood still. She listened at the door for a moment and heard nothing so opened it carefully to see if anyone was there. There was no one in sight so she opened the door a little wider to be sure that the whole room was empty. Her father had hauled Jimmy outside and nearly beat him to death.

There was no one there to comfort her; she was only six years old, alone and very frightened. She was so ashamed and frightened and knew she had to hide this. She looked back at the bed and saw the blanket all stained with blood, her blood. Miriam pulled the bloody blanket off the bed and carried it into the kitchen to get the brush, the big bar of Sunlight soap and a pail of water to scrub it clean. She knew how to clean bloodstains; her father was a trapper. She scrubbed that blanket until her arms went numb and she hung it on the line outside to dry. She took off her nightgown, put on some clothes and climbed into bed with her little sisters. No one, not Miriam or her father, ever spoke about the rape; he had taken care of it in his own way and it was to be forgotten. It would be more than twenty years before she ever told anyone about it.

As she got older, Miriam started to understand why her mother was always so eager to get out of the house to go to work. Patrick had become a violent drinker and Annie would complain about his drinking and that would send him around the bend. They would fight; he would beat her and she would leave. Miriam and the other kids would hide as soon as the fighting started but they would always peek out and watch the whole thing, afraid for their mother's safety. Patrick got to the point where he would drink anything; home brew, aftershave, hairspray, mouthwash, perfume. At first Annie hid her precious little bottles of cheap perfume from him but he always beat it out of her to find where it was hidden so he could drink it. The cheapest perfume had the highest alcohol content and she couldn't afford the better stuff, so she just quit buying any perfume altogether. It wasn't worth the beatings.

At six years old, Miriam was considered old enough to look after her two younger sisters, aged two and four. They called her Little Mother. She looked after them as well as a six year old could and helped keep the house clean; doing dishes and laundry. One night, after she had cleaned up all the dishes and her father started slapping her mother around in his usual drunken stupor, she just couldn't take it anymore and ran to get the broom to help her mother defend herself. Miriam thrust the broom over at her mother and she grabbed onto it with both hands and rammed the handle end of it into her father's shoulder. Patrick responded to the pain in his shoulder dropping back and turning away momentarily. Annie took advantage of his temporary distraction and rammed the broom handle into his back as hard as she could two or three times more before he turned around and saw that she meant business. Miriam had tried in vain to get away from the battle but was caught in between them now and found herself in the middle of a tug-of-war over the broom. When they finally noticed her crying between them, they let go and ran out of the house, still fighting, with Annie in control of the broom once again. Miriam fell to the floor in a little heap, a worn out, frightened child. She cried through the night and the next day a heavy fog moved in on her world.

Without a word to anyone, Annie had taken the flight south; packed up a suitcase and left; abandoned them all. In response, Patrick went on a bender that seemed like it would never end.

When it became clear that Annie would not return, Annie's mother stepped in and took over care of the children, but she was very old and her health was not good. Eventually, Grandmother decided the best thing for the kids would be to send them to foster homes off the reserve; she just could not look after them anymore and their father was of no use to them now. The kids were all placed in foster homes down south in different towns with language being a big problem for some, especially Miriam's brothers who had never learned to speak English because they spent all their time with their father on the trap line. This would make life extremely difficult for them. Miriam, however, managed to ease through the culture shock of moving into a town with white people but she still missed her family.

The foster home Miriam was sent to wasn't really that much different than her real home. Her foster father was a daily drinker and her foster mother was a cold, distant woman, always too busy for the kids. It was a huge old boarding house and there were other Dene and Cree students from up north boarding there as well as some white children. Things were always changing at the house, kids moving out, kids moving in. It wasn't what you could call a normal childhood for any of them except for the fact that they all attended school.

By the time Miriam got to high school, she had become obsessed with her weight, but she really loved to eat and she would eat and eat until she could hold no more and then force herself to vomit. Bingeing and purging worked well to keep the weight down. Part of this focus on staying thin had come from her foster mother's influence. She was always on some diet or another, using gimmicks that she ordered from television commercials like the blow-up girdle that promised to whittle your waist down with its' sauna-like effect or the little plastic turntable that you stood on and twisted yourself around. She was a sucker for all of the gadgets and magic potions that promised to make you instantly svelte with little or no effort and she was so concerned with her own appearance that she never really noticed what the foster kids were up to.

Miriam started drinking with her friends in grade ten; they were the underdogs who had been drawn together and they drank to get drunk every chance they got. Even though she was missing more and more school; too hung over to move some mornings, Miriam held her honor roll status for one more year. After that, her marks went down steadily. Still, she managed to graduate from grade twelve, but just barely. When she applied for university, she just made the minimum average required for entrance.

Once Miriam started university and was away from her foster mother's constant reminder that staying thin was paramount in one's life, she began to lose interest in her physical activities one by one. When the weight started creeping on, she tried starving herself but could not withstand that for long, and finally just accepted the numbers. At university, drinking was definitely still the best way to have a good time and kill your appetite at the same time, so she drank whenever she could throughout the weekdays, always binge drinking on the weekends. The weekends were what she lived for. It was always the same; get drunk, blackout and have a bad hangover the next day, sometimes so wicked that she would vow to never drink again, ever. But as the days went by and she felt better she would start looking forward to the weekend binge and do it all over again.

It was a miracle that she managed to stay in university as long as she did. Her ability to cram for exams saved her because it was getting harder and harder to retain much of anything that she was supposedly learning but it all caught up to her when she got kicked out in the middle of her third year. She was shocked and amazed that they could do this to her even though she was completely aware that her grades were terrible and the faculty knew all about her drinking. She cried over it for a few days and then shook it off. "Who gives a shit about that anyway" she told her friend Roberta and good friend that she was, Roberta dropped out of school right then and there as a show of support for her best friend.

Their student funding was cut off within a month so they both went on social assistance and decided they were just going to enjoy themselves from then on. They rented a tiny apartment downtown where they could walk to all the skid row bars they decided they wanted to hang around in. Drugs like speed or acid were as easy to get as booze but they only took a few trips before they decided it was too scary for them. The first time they scored LSD they were just sitting in the bar with their draft beers lined up on the little round table when some guy offered them two tiny little pills in exchange for the six draft.

Miriam looked at Roberta and shrugged her shoulders "Why not eh?"

Roberta said "Sure let's go for it" and the two little pills replaced the six tall glasses on the table.

They swallowed the pills and waited. Soon the world was an incredible new place; amazingly weird and wild and they left the dingy bar to enjoy the trip. They made it back to the apartment and decided LSD was the greatest until it started to wear off. Coming down was another story. The hallucinations were terrifying. Miriam was exhausted, sitting at the kitchen table staring at the stove when something caught her attention. The stove was changing right before her eyes! She tried to call Roberta to come and see this but she was so scared she couldn't speak. Her eyes were drawn to the stove and its' morphing form. It was moving slowly as if it were breathing. It was alive! She watched the stove breathe for a while and as the fear mounted in her, she closed her eyes to shut it out. But what she saw with her eyes closed was even worse. In her head there was a pounding, groaning sound and all she could see and feel were the flames of Hell. The sound was telling her this. The flames were everywhere; red and purple and yellow and the heat was so intense she thought she would faint. When she opened her eyes, the stove was still there but it wasn't breathing anymore. She let her head drop onto her folded arms on the table and fell into a deep sleep, not moving until the next morning. That wasn't enough though to stop her from trying it a few more times before it scared her enough to quit and stick to booze. She got tired of beer and switched to red wine; the taste of red wine was heavenly but the hangovers were deadly. After a good red wine binge she would wake up with a pounding headache feeling as though her head would explode. She tried hard liquor but the blackouts were worse so she went back to beer and red wine.

Miriam was becoming bored and restless with the bar life and decided to accept an offer from her foster sister Betty to come and live with her in Iqaluit in the Arctic. Betty needed a babysitter and it seemed like good timing for Miriam. She loved the Arctic; it was more like home than the city she had been living in. Miriam managed to find paying jobs here and there besides babysitting; one stint as a personal care attendant at a care home and some part-time clerical work at the town administration office, but as soon as she had any money, she spent it on liquor. It got so that she couldn't even get through the days that she babysat without drinking and the nights out at the bar had become a steady blur of blackouts.

Around this time, Miriam began to see a therapist where she started talking about her birth mother and her foster mother. She told the therapist she had no real recollection of her birth mother and no feelings toward her. The therapist told her this was a memory block; that she really did have these memories inside of her somewhere, but she was holding them back because it was just too painful. That barrier could be opened up though, if she were willing to relinquish her survival tool of denial. It was easy to admit that her foster mother never loved her; that she was only taking care of her for the money, but it still hurt. As she started opening up to her feelings, a friend introduced her to the Bahai faith. Miriam was attracted by their philosophy of one world one religion and she joined; it seemed to be what she needed to fill the void but even Bahaullah could not stop her from drinking.

When she had been in Iqaluit for just over two years, she was hired for one of the sought after federal government jobs everyone wanted. On her first day of work, Miriam was nowhere to be found. She had a sudden urge to return to her reserve and it was such a strong pull that she did not question it, just packed up to take the next plane out of Iqaluit headed for Toronto.

When she arrived in Toronto, she had a change of heart and decided to stay in the city, go back to university and complete her degree in social work. Things went back to the way they were before, trying to get through school between the hangovers and the blackouts.

While she was back at university, Miriam began to experience depressions and sought out a psychiatrist who diagnosed her as clinically depressed and prescribed Prozac. She had a boyfriend at the time and surprisingly found herself pregnant. She told her psychiatrist that she did not want the baby; she was so depressed that she wanted to die, so why in the world would she want to bring a child into the same world that she herself wanted to leave. The doctor arranged a therapeutic abortion and Miriam went through with it. This proved to be some sort of a turning point for Miriam. She decided to seriously try sobriety after her doctor diagnosed her with diabetes and warned her of the complications associated with alcohol. The way she was living had no rewards for her anymore and she decided to join a Pentecostal church where she put all her energy into being a good Christian.

Miriam attended AA meetings off and on but couldn't seem to commit. Her lack of commitment resulted in regular forays into binge drinking again and again, always finding someone or something to blame; the friends who wouldn't leave her alone; the friends who just wanted to have some fun, or the friends who had died so tragically.

Miriam remains on the edge; out there somewhere, taking the risk that one more binge might be her last, not yet ready to come in from the cold. Say a little prayer for Miriam.

The End

# CHAPTER NINE
# HOLLY

The woman lying in the hospital bed was not happy and for good reason. Her abdomen was distended to the point where it had become impossible for her to sit, so she had been placed in a semi-prone position to ease her discomfort. Dr. Edelman, the Internal Medicine Specialist on staff at the hospital, had come in to take a sample of whatever it was that was filling her up like a water balloon by inserting a long, hollow needle into her belly directly below her navel. The doctor said that he could drain it but then it would simply fill up again each time it was drained, so there really wasn't much point in putting the patient through the distress and discomfort of the procedure. Liz's ankles had begun to fill up with fluid about a year earlier but she had dismissed it as she usually did with health problems, always wearing pants to hide the swelling. She kept quiet about a lot of things; didn't want anyone snooping into her life. When she lost control of her bodily functions and could not get out of bed because of the distended abdomen, her husband panicked and called the ambulance that brought her to the hospital where she would spend her last days.

Watching someone die of alcoholic cirrhosis of the liver is not something you soon forget. It is an extremely painful, lingering death, a death that can be prevented. Liz didn't have to die like that; it didn't have to happen that way, but it did. She just couldn't stop drinking no matter what; not even to save her own life.

After she had been in the hospital for about a week, Dr. Edelman asked her "How much do you drink Liz?"

No answer from the patient.

The doctor looked over at the high back chair where Liz's daughter Holly was sitting and continued "Twenty ounces a day for the past fifty years, does that sound about right?"

Holly suddenly realized that he was aiming the question at her, glanced over at her mother and slowly nodded her head in agreement "Yeah, that's probably about right".

Liz turned her face away from both of them and, looking into the curtain, attempted to defend herself "Oh, no, not that much".

The doctor started moving toward the door with her chart in his hand "Oh, I think that's pretty accurate Liz. All your health problems are because of alcohol" and walked out of the room; a doctor who had obviously seen far too many people drink themselves to death.

Liz slowly turned her gaze toward the big vinyl chair.

Holly looked at her through a smudge of tears "But you don't deserve to die in so much pain."

"Well maybe I do, I did this to myself. I was stupid."

Holly gets up to leave the room as a loud sigh comes from the bed and Liz appears to fall asleep.

By some miracle, Dr. Edelman is still in the hallway working on charts. The odds of talking to a doctor most days is like seeing a unicorn, so she quickly walks over to the chart station where he is busy writing on a blue sheet of paper to ask him what the prognosis is for her mother.

"I just want to know the truth. She's dying isn't she?"

The doctor keeps on writing, not looking up as he speaks "It doesn't look good; her condition is very advanced. All we can do now is try and make her comfortable"; hands the paper to a nurse and walks away.

Liz goes in and out of consciousness with the lucid intervals becoming less frequent every day over the following weeks and Holly's eyes are raw and burning from crying. Holly and her sister Danielle are there day and night as much as they possibly can be, and Danielle seems to hold out some hope that their mother will eventually come out of the hospital. Holly sees nothing but death as she watches Liz reaching her arms up to the sky, her sickly yellow eyes pleading to some unseen thing "Hurry Hurry Quick Quick" as if it could just lift her out of there and take her away from this misery.

Liz refused all nutrition after a couple of weeks in the hospital and her condition progressed to a semi-comatose state aided by morphine patches. The last twenty-four hours must have been Hell for her because she moaned loudly as though in great pain until the death rattle began and Danielle and Holly urged her on.

"Let go Mum, just let go and you'll see all your old boyfriends. You'll see them all again and there'll be a party for you. It's okay, just let go!" They were alone with her when she gasped her last breath and they said goodbye to their mother.

As far back as Holly could remember there was booze in her world. Her father was an alcoholic who got hauled away by the police for the last time when she was five years old. She could still remember hanging on to her mother's dress crying after one of the neighbors had called the police to come and pick him up. This wasn't the first time he had passed out in the back alley and they were fed up with him. After he was gone, Holly wasn't supposed to ever talk about him again. Liz told her that if anyone asked, she should say that she didn't have a Dad and that's all. Of course, all the kids asked "Where's your Dad?" and her response was always the same "I don't have a Dad". Some of the neighborhood kids weren't allowed to play with Holly and Danielle because they didn't have a Dad. Single, working mothers were assumed to be bad women.

Occasionally over the years when he was in town, their father phoned Holly and told her to bring Danielle and come downtown to meet him. They would catch a bus to get downtown to the seedy men's hotel where he always stayed, visit for a short while, then take the bus back home and never tell their mother about the visits because according to her, he didn't even exist.

Liz loved to party and she had lots of partying friends. She had a great sense of humor when she was sober but after a few drinks it went sour and she would spit cruel remarks and insults at her children in particular. There was rarely an encouraging comment for the girls; it was more often than not "What do you want to do that for? You'll never be any good at it!" "You'll never pass, you'll never win, you'll never be any good at anything!" "You'll never be a good mother. I hope you have kids as bad as you!" Holly drew inward as a child without many friends and Danielle surrounded herself with them all the time; both trying to be okay in their own way.

When the kids were too young to stay on their own, Liz would ship them off to their grandparents' farm every chance she got. They spent all the school holidays there including most of the summers. When they were at the farm, their Grandfather was constantly playing what he considered jokes on them. He thought it nothing short of hilarious to get them to hold out a hand with eyes closed as he would place some grotesque object like a duck's head, a pig's foot, a live frog or something equally frightening into their hands. They fell for it every time. He once told them to go down to the basement to get him a jar of jam out of the cold storage room. When they got down to the bottom of the stairs, the light went out.

Holly yelled back up the stairs "It's dark down here Grandpa! I can't see anything!"

He yelled back, sounding angry, "Just pull the light string in the middle of the room!" They inched forward in the darkness, Holly reaching up as high as she could, flailing her arms side to side to feel for the string with Danielle right behind her. At last, she felt the string and gave it a good yank. They were both looking up as the light came on and shone directly on a severed pig's head hanging just to the side of the light bulb. They both screamed, turned around and ran back up the stairs tripping over each other as they went. Grandpa was still sitting there in the kitchen and looked over as they fell into the doorway.

"What's the matter with you two, where's my jam?" he bellowed.

For grade one show and tell, Grandpa gave Danielle an aborted pig fetus in a glass jar to take to school. When she proudly showed the teacher what she had brought, the teacher recoiled in horror and forbade her from showing the class. It was just one gross, scary thing after another. When they were back home in the city, Liz, Holly and Danielle lived in a little two-bedroom wartime house where for many years all three shared one double bed while the other room was either rented out or occupied by some live-in babysitter who rarely got paid. There was a string of old women who came to live with them when they were younger while Liz went to work, horrible old women mostly, especially Mrs. Cooper. She was a short, dumpy woman with sparse, frizzy red hair which she would tie up with a scarf that she stole from Holly and lock them out of the house until just before their mother was due to come home from work everyday. Mrs. Cooper's grandson Neil appeared one day; a boy of about twelve with a suitcase and a pet monkey he called Jimbo. Mrs. Cooper begged Liz to let him stay just until she found him somewhere else, so Neil and his stinky monkey moved into the cold, damp basement where there was an old cot with a dip in the middle of it near the coal furnace. They lasted about a week until the nasty little creature bit Mrs. Cooper. They disappeared shortly after that; the whole bunch of them; Holly's scarf and all.

By the time she reached high school, Holly hung around mainly with kids who drank and smoked and had drugs. She always managed to earn enough money to buy what she wanted and there was always a way to get booze and drugs. Danielle was growing up and away from

Holly; she had her own friends and they were getting into their own kind of trouble, especially stealing. It got to the point where the two sisters had nothing to do with each other anymore and if they did, it was good for a fight.

Liz focused most of her attention on male friends so Holly and Danielle both avoided being home anymore than they had to. If a boy was picking her up to go out on a date, Holly would try and meet him outside the house so that her mother couldn't embarrass her in front of him as she had done every time she invited someone in. Holly swore that she did not want to be like her mother but still she drank and before long, there were mornings when she could not remember anything about the night before; where she had been, with who or what she had done. But everybody seemed to think that blacking out was a big joke and apparently, passing out was nothing to worry about either, so she just tried not to worry about it.

Holly was managing to get through high school but at the end of grade eleven she decided she might as well just quit and get a full-time job to make more money. Her mother thought that was a great idea because it would mean that she could move out on her own then. One of her teachers did not agree that this was such a good idea though and secured a bursary for Holly to complete grade twelve and she graduated with a business education certificate without ever attending a Monday morning or

Friday afternoon class. By now she was drinking regularly and no one seemed to notice; at least they didn't say anything if they did. There wasn't an occasion that didn't call for drinking; she even drank to get ready to go out drinking. She drank alone too which did not seem odd to her at all. She did a lot of things alone so why would drinking be any different; it was impossible to convince other people to do the things she wanted to do, so it was just easier to keep to herself. She had gotten into regular pot smoking and using speed by now as well. It was cheap and easy to get. This was the sixties, peace, love and drugs.

Holly was obsessed with the notion of traveling and seeing the world, so working three or four jobs at a time, she managed to save up enough money to buy airfare to London with a whole hundred and forty dollars left over. It was hard to save money. She left the country not knowing if or when she would be back and there she was on a plane to London; a skinny 18 year old in a clingy pink jumpsuit with a hundred and forty dollars to her name. She was not scared but she was crying, and she really didn't know why; she was just so sad and she didn't actually have a plan; only that she was on her way. Her mother had asked her when she was coming back and all she could tell her was that she didn't know. The only regret she had was leaving her little sister.

When the plane landed in London, she exchanged some of her travelers' cheques for British Sterling and cashed in the refundable portion of her return airline ticket. She then located the buses all lined up outside the airport to take passengers into the city and dragged her heavy red backpack with the Canadian Flag stitched onto it over to a bus headed for London Center. The bus dropped her off near a Victorian bedsit that she had found on the bulletin board at the airport.

The clerk at the desk of the bedsit took her money and pointed to a stairway. Suddenly, the exhaustion hit her. She hadn't slept for three days with all the going away parties and she barely made it to the room before she conked out.

By the end of the next day, Holly had moved in to a cheaper residential hotel and had her first job working in a typing pool at an insurance company. The temporary placement agency said they could find her as much work as she wanted which was a good thing because the hundred and forty dollars was half gone already. She worked a few temp jobs until she landed a permanent cashier position at a restaurant called Eskalade. Then she responded to an ad on the bulletin board at the laundrette near Eskalade for roommates and moved into a flat in Earls Court with six other foreigners. The flat was cold and damp and had a little step-up closet with a tub in the hallway and coin-operated electricity and gas meters. It was more or less a continuous party between the flat and the pubs with lots of drugs and cheap wine.

Holly dove into the party scene with enthusiasm and the blackouts increased. She was becoming a danger to herself and to others at times and it scared her to death whenever she allowed herself to really think about it. She promised herself over and over that it wouldn't happen again but it always did. She was becoming paranoid of running into people that she might have been with the night before or some other night before; some night when she had done something stupid like knock over an aquarium, cry through a dinner party, fall down a flight of stairs or just make a scene in any one of the countless stupid ways she could have. The paranoia was very uncomfortable and sometimes she even thought the police were after her, even though she had no idea why they would be.

London was exciting but it was time to move on, so Holly decided to pack up and head south to the resort town of Torquay where she had a job within hours as a chambermaid; a job which she knew nothing about. She was a terrible chambermaid and was soon transferred into the restaurant. When she got tired of Torquay, she began answering want ads for all kinds of jobs in Europe and took an au pair position in Florence where she lived in a marble penthouse with three children and their parents who wanted the kids to learn to speak English. The job was hell with slave labor wages, but the city was amazing and there was a lot of wine. After a few months, she grew more and more depressed, decided the au pair life was not for her and made her way back to London to regroup.

Back at the Harlequin Hotel in London, it was great to see friends again and that was how it went for the next couple of years, back and forth from Europe to London between jobs. The longest job stint was at the Student Travel Bureau in Athens. The job was good because she could earn commission and she was in demand for the tourists who spoke only English. She rented a little room not far from where she worked where she could actually look up out of the courtyard and see the Acropolis when it was lit up at night. The nearby Plaka was always alive with music where the Retsina wine was cheap and life was good for a while. This was by far the most beautiful place she had ever been but she couldn't stay.

Everywhere she went something was always nagging at her to move along. One of the Australian girls from the flat in Earls Court was still in London when she got back from Athens, and the two of them decided to head to Morocco. Holly usually traveled alone but they were told that young women, especially fair-haired young women, should not travel to Morocco alone because of the white slave trade. They spent a couple of months touring around, staying at twenty-five cent a night hostels with no toilet facilities, eating at street stalls out of huge round pots and smoking lots of the local keifur. When they both ran out of money, they headed for Spain where Judith had a friend. After about three days of intense showering they decided to stay in Malaga for a while and try to get some work tutoring English. Then Judith fell in love so Holly moved on. Back and forth again, a job here, a job there; make enough money to move on.

There were occasional letters from Liz and Danielle. The letters were rarely encouraging; things were bad, Danielle wrote, Mum was drinking heavily and they were fighting a lot. Mum had another new boyfriend she met at work and they were talking about getting married. Danielle was really upset about this because it had been decided that she couldn't live with them when they got married and they were expecting Holly to come back so that Danielle could live with her. This was breaking Holly's heart, poor little Danielle was the one person in the whole world she really cared about. After reading one of Danielle's letters, she was so preoccupied that she stepped off a curb as a car whizzed by so close that it actually tore off one of her coat buttons. That did it. She decided right then and there that she would go back for Danielle.

As usual, she had no money; so she wrote her mother and asked for help with the ticket. Her mother told her that she couldn't come up with that much money so Holly stayed in London and worked for another two months squirreling away every penny she could to save up the fare home. It was so sad to leave London; it had become just like home to her and it broke her heart to leave all her friends but she had to go for Danielle.

The family seemed happy to see her. She had lots of stories to tell and she had little gifts for everyone. Liz moved in with Gerard after the wedding and it was made clear that Holly and Danielle were not welcome to live there. They didn't get along well; none of them; not one combination of any of them seemed to be able to get along, and it wasn't long before Holly couldn't stand it any more and left with a guy she met at a bar. Tim was a U.S. Marine deserter; a conscientious objector to the Vietnam war. Danielle now had no choice but to go and stay with her mother and new stepfather. They treated her badly and she reacted badly. Her room was a cot in the laundry room in the basement under the rack of clothes. The fighting escalated between Danielle and Liz.

Holly and Tim headed north to Inuvik in the North West Territories where she got a job in a lounge and worked nights serving drinks then partied till morning at the trailer where all the serving staff lived. After about a year of Arctic life, Holly was feeling so guilty about leaving Danielle that she sublet an apartment in Edmonton and sent for her to come and live with her and Tim.

Holly had started thinking about her father when she went up north, the father she hadn't seen in more than a dozen years. Liz had never actually divorced her first husband because he had just disappeared to the world. When she prepared to marry Gerard, she had to acquire a declaration from the RCMP to state that her husband could not be found, allowing them to declare him dead for legal purposes so that she could re-marry. Holly knew he wasn't dead though; they just hadn't looked in the right places. She asked about him everywhere she went and found a couple of people up north who said he had been there at some point but had moved on, so she kept on searching. Back in Edmonton, she started by calling the Salvation Army shelters and lo and behold he had been at one of them in the past year. They said he showed up occasionally so she should try back again. The next time she called, he was there. Her heart skipped a beat, now what? Without eve thinking, she grabbed her coat and headed for the shelter.

She got to the front door and went up to the counter asking to see Arne Arnason.

"Yeah, he's in, just a minute, I'll go get him".

In another minute, there he was, standing in the doorway looking at her like she was a stranger. She barely recognized the old man standing there. He shouldn't be so old, she thought to herself, he was only fifty something, but here was this very old man, somewhat familiar, looking back at her. He was thin, really thin, and his once curly blonde hair had gone to some kind of non-colored fuzz. He coughed a couple of times; a deep chest rattle cough; the echo of a million cigarettes.

As if he might be hard of hearing, Holly loudly and slowly articulated "Dad, it's me Holly, your daughter!"

He looked at her, moved in closer very slowly and in a raspy voice, quietly said "Well, Jesus Christ! What are you doing here?" No hug, no embrace, not even a handshake. Holly faltered a little and cleared her throat to explain how she had been looking for him for a long time, that no one seemed to know where he was.

"Yeah well, I don't keep in touch much". They sat down at a card table in the TV room and faced each other awkwardly; he with his nicotine stained fingers clasped tightly in front of him on the table.

"Mum got married again you know. The RCMP couldn't find you but here you are eh?" She did most of the talking which wasn't a whole lot, but he didn't seem to be all that interested in reminiscing much about anything. The fact was that he couldn't remember a whole lot; either the booze had wiped out his memory or he had erased it himself. They visited for a few more minutes and when the silence became unbearable, she left, leaving him her address and inviting him to come for supper at her apartment the next day at six o'clock.

He showed up about an hour early the next day half frozen from the walk. It was winter and all he wore was a thin old suit jacket; no hat, no gloves and when he took off his shoes at the door, he had one bright pink fuzzy sock and one dark one. She couldn't help but try and make a joke of the socks to which he replied with a grin.

"Well I washed my socks and hung them up on the line to dry at the shelter there and someone stole them and these were the only two left so I took 'em."

Her heart was shattering. She told him to come in and take a chair in the kitchen where she was starting to prepare something for their supper. He sat down facing the fridge and when she opened it, his eye fixed on the one lone bottle of beer sitting there. She looked from the beer to him and back and handed it to him without a word. He opened it with the opener she gave him and poured it down his throat in one long swig. That was all the liquor she had in the house at the moment but if there had been another bottle in there, she would have been doing the same. After supper she decided she just could not let him leave the way he was dressed and took a pair of Tim's thick socks and his old army jacket out of the closet and insisted her father take them.

"Tim can get another, no problem" she assured him. Arne quickly pulled on the coat, mumbled thanks a few times and left. It was hard, that reunion. He couldn't seem to remember her name. He kept calling her by his sister's name.

Just before he died a few years later, he told Holly that he never should have had kids and he meant it just like that, matter of fact. The ultimate rejection, or maybe his way of making an amend to her? He had chosen his path and maybe she shouldn't have interfered. He didn't indicate that he was happy that she had made the effort to find him or that he actually ever wanted to be part of her life. He seemed to be content to walk out the door again and never look back. He managed to stay alive for a few more years living on the streets but the good Samaritans who look out for street people decided at some point that he was in danger of dying or being killed out there so they found him a rehab care home. His health was bad, having had several heart attacks and broken the same leg so many times that it wouldn't heal properly anymore. The care home was a sort of retirement rehab center that he qualified for because he had once been in the air force. He was admitted on the condition that he sober up and stay sober. He went in a sick, broken man and attended the AA meetings they held there daily and died sober a few years later from bone cancer. After he died, Holly and Danielle went to the care home to collect his meager belongings.

The attendant picked up his box of stuff, held out a battered old copy of the blue Alcoholics Anonymous book, looked straight at Holly and said "Here, you should have this."

Holly was so insulted "Why me, she thought, why is she saying that I should have it? The nerve of her!" They took the box back home and Holly told Danielle to keep the book; she didn't want it.

Tim had gone back to the states and she never heard from him again; maybe he got arrested. Danielle had moved on with her own life so Holly drank alone again. One night at a party, she met a guy who seemed pretty nice; he made her laugh and she needed a few laughs so she gave him her phone number and he called and called and called. Mason was always either on the phone or on the doorstep. It was more of a stalking than a dating relationship but she was so sad and alone that she was actually flattered with all the attention. No one had been that consumed with her ever before and she actually kind of liked it. In no time at all he had moved in and they partied together for about a year before she got pregnant.

She was ecstatic about the baby; she had never really even thought about having a baby but this was going to be amazing; she would love this little baby like nobody had ever loved before. They would be good parents and they would never desert this baby. For the first time, she had a reason not to drink or do drugs. From the minute she found out she was pregnant, she abstained from everything that might be bad for the baby except cigarettes. She still smoked cigarettes; her doctor even smoked cigarettes at their appointments and never said that it would be bad for the baby. Holly even managed to abstain from alcohol through the first six months of the baby's life while she was breast feeding, all the while knowing and planning when she could drink again. But that plan got put on hold while she had another baby.

Holly had never known such happiness before. Being a mother to these two beautiful babies was easily the best thing that had ever happened in her life but Mason was now drinking heavily and staying out later and later all the time and getting in trouble with the law, so things were never worse in that way. He blamed Holly for everything that went wrong; everything in the entire universe was her fault; everything that happened to him was her fault. He started accusing her of sleeping with other men, which she wasn't. The fact was that he was the one who was sleeping around. His job as a salesman took him on the road with no shortage of hotel nights. The more he cheated on Holly, the nastier he got. He was loud, mean and obnoxious when he was drunk and it got so that Holly was convinced that nothing she could do was right and she started drinking again to cope. She tried not to drink until the kids were asleep and she was pretty good at controlling the timing of her drinking but as time went on, the need to numb the pain overtook all reason and her drinking was out of control again.

She tried to leave Mason five times and every time, he would come crying to her that they were meant to be together for life and he would change. Yes he would change; he swore on a bible that he would change and everything would be better if she would please just give him one more chance. When she decided she had enough, she asked Mason to leave for good. He refused so she called a lawyer and obtained a legal separation. Mason managed to convince all their friends and family that she was responsible for the breakup; that she had cheated and lied and that she was an uncontrollable drunk. He had even brainwashed the kids to believe his poison.

The drunk part was the only truth about Holly and one night as she sat drinking by herself, she decided that she could not go on like this any longer. She was worn out from the pain and the booze did nothing to kill it anymore. She called the number in the phone book for Alcoholics Anonymous. The voice at the other end asked her if she would like someone to come over and talk to her and she said okay, hoping to herself that this was the right thing to do. After she hung up the phone she hid the big jug of red wine she had been drinking and tried to make herself look presentable. Two women showed up at her front door and she took them into the kitchen where she sat down with them, her face puffy from crying.

"Don't worry, everything will be just fine, have you got a cup of coffee?" They sat and smoked cigarettes and drank coffee for hours while they told their stories, how their lives had been ruined by alcohol and how they had come out of it with the help of AA. They seemed to really want to help her so when they offered to take her to an AA meeting the next night she agreed. After they left, Holly retrieved the jug of wine from the cupboard where she had stashed it and proceeded to finish drinking it, somehow knowing it would be her last.

The next night they showed up as promised and took her to the meeting. It was a ladies meeting and there were dozens of women there, all kinds of women, and they seemed to be happy; having a good time laughing and joking with each other. Everyone was sitting down with little ashtrays in their hands when the meeting was called to order with a prayer and immediately, Holly thought "Oh shit! This is some religious crap, what am I doing here? I can't do this!" But she was so broken and desperate to feel something other than what she had that she stayed glued to her seat at the back of the room. She was really hung over from the night before so her brain was muddled, but something got through and at some point during the meeting, she felt herself decide that she would just sit there and listen and do whatever it was they said to do because they said if you want what we have, just do what we do. They said that it was a spiritual program and you could choose your own higher power and they spoke about God.

A kind of calm came over her, it was somehow okay; she didn't need to argue and question everything anymore; she could just accept and believe. It was such a huge job being in control of everything, maybe it would be good to leave that up to someone else. Sitting in the back of that room, shaking like a leaf and terrified to look at anyone, Holly felt, to her amazement, for the first time in her life, that she belonged somewhere. She had never, in her entire life, felt that she belonged anywhere, never felt comfortable, always felt like a freak, different from everyone else. Here they didn't judge or blame her and she felt hopeful. She left that meeting knowing her life had changed; she could feel it in her soul. She didn't want the meeting to end; the first hour of peace she had ever felt was too good to lose. Holly learned to overcome her fear and pain and never looked back from that day on.

The End

Printed in the United States
137927LV00001B/1/P